Anonymous

Stories by American Authors

Anonymous

Stories by American Authors

ISBN/EAN: 9783744750844

Printed in Europe, USA, Canada, Australia, Japan

Cover: Foto ©Andreas Hilbeck / pixelio.de

More available books at **www.hansebooks.com**

Stories by
American Authors

IX.

MARSE CHAN.
By Thomas Nelson Page.

MR. BIXBY'S CHRISTMAS VISITOR.
By Charles S. Gage.

ELI.
By C. H. White.

YOUNG STRONG OF "THE CLARION."
By Milicent Washburn Shinn.

HOW OLD WIGGINS WORE SHIP.
By Captain Roland T. Coffin.

"—MAS HAS COME."
By Leonard Kip.

NEW YORK
CHARLES SCRIBNER'S SONS
1885

MARSE CHAN.

A TALE OF OLD VIRGINIA.

By Thomas Nelson Page.

ONE afternoon, in the autumn of 1872, I was riding leisurely down the sandy road that winds along the top of the water-shed between two of the smaller rivers of eastern Virginia. The road I was travelling, following "the ridge" for miles, had just struck me as most significant of the character of the race whose only avenue of communication with the outside world it had formerly been. Their once splendid mansions, now fast falling to decay, appeared to view from time to time, set back far from the road, in proud seclusion among groves of oak and hickory now scarlet and gold with the early frost. Distance was nothing to this people; time was of no consequence to them. They desired but a level path in life, and that they

⁎ *Century Magazine, April,* 1884.

had, though the way was longer and the outer world strode by them as they dreamed.

I was aroused from my reflections by hearing some one ahead of me calling, " Heah !—heah—whoo-oop, heah !"

Turning the curve in the road, I saw just before me a negro standing, with a hoe and a watering-pot in his hand. He had evidently just gotten over the " worm-fence " into the road, out of the path which led zigzag across the " old field " and was lost to sight in the dense growth of sassafras. When I rode up, he was looking anxiously back down this path for his dog. So engrossed was he that he did not even hear my horse, and 1 reined in to wait until he should turn around and satisfy my curiosity as to the handsome old place half a mile off from the road.

The numerous out-buildings and the large barns and stables told that it had once been the seat of wealth, and the wild waste of sassafras that covered the broad fields gave it an air of desolation that greatly excited my interest. Entirely oblivious of my proximity, the negro went on calling, " Whoo-oop, heah !" until along the path, walking very slowly and with great dignity, appeared a noble-looking old orange and white setter, gray with age, and corpulent with excessive feeding. As soon as he came in sight, his master began :

" Yes, dat you ! You gittin' deaf as well as bline, I s'pose ! Kyarnt heah me callin', I reckon ? Whyn't yo' come on, dawg ?"

The setter sauntered slowly up to the fence and stopped without even deigning a look at the speaker, who immediately proceeded to take the rails down, talking meanwhile :

" Now, I got to pull down de gap, I s'pose ! Yo' so sp'ilt yo' kyahn' hardly walk. Jes' ez able to git over it as I is ! Jes' like white folks—t'ink 'cuz you's white and I's black, I got to wait on yo' all de time. Ne'm mine, I ain' gwi' do it !"

The fence having been pulled down sufficiently low to suit his dogship, he marched sedately through, and, with a hardly perceptible lateral movement of his tail, walked on down the road. Putting up the rails carefully, the negro turned and saw me. -

" Sarvent, marster," he said, taking his hat off. Then, as if apologetically for having permitted a stranger to witness what was merely a family affair, he added : " He know I don' mean nothin' by what I sez. He's Marse Chan's dawg, an' he's so ole he kyahn git long no pearter. He know I'se jes' prodjickin' wid 'im."

" Who is Marse Chan ?" I asked ; " and whose place is that over there—and the one a mile or two back—the place with the big gate and the carved stone pillars ?"

" Marse Chan," said the darkey, " he's Marse Channin'—my young marster ; an' dem places—dis one's Weall's, an' de one back dyar wid de rock gate-pos's is ole Cun'l Chahmb'lin's. Dey don' nobody live dyar now, 'cep' niggers. Arfter

de war some one or nudder bought our place, but
his name done kind o' slipped me. I nuvver hearn
on 'im befo'; I think dey's half-strainers. I don'
ax none on 'em no odds. I lives down de road
heah, a little piece, an' I jes' steps down of a evenin' and looks arfter de graves."

"Well, where is Marse Chan?" I asked.

"Hi! don' you know? Marse Chan, he went
in de army. I wuz wid 'im. Yo' know he warn'
gwine an' lef' Sam."

"Will you tell me all about it?" I said, dis-
mounting.

Instantly, and as if by instinct, the darky
stepped forward and took my bridle. I demurred a
little; but with a bow that would have honored
old Sir Roger, he shortened the reins, and taking
my horse from me, led him along.

"Now tell me about Marse Chan," I said.

"Lawd, marster, hit's so long ago, I'd a'most
forgit all about it, ef I hedn' been wid him ever
sence he wuz born. Ez 'tis, I remembers it jes'
like 'twuz yistiddy. Yo' know Marse Chan an'
me—we wuz boys togedder. I wuz older'n he
wuz, jes' de same ez he wuz whiter'n me. I wuz
born plantin' corn time, de spring arfter big Jim
an' de six steers got washed away at de upper ford
right down dyar b'low de quarters ez he wuz a
bringin' de Chris'mas things home; an' Marse
Chan, he warn' born tell mos' to der harves' arfter
my sister Nancy married Cun'l Chahmb'lin's
Torm, 'bout eight years arfterwoods.

" Well, when Marse Chan wuz born dey wuz de grettes' doin's at home you ever did see.   De folks all hed holiday, jes' like in de Chris'mas.   Ole marster (we didn' call 'im *ole* marster tell arfter Marse Chan wuz born—befo' dat he wuz jes' de marster, so)—well, ole marster, his face fyar shine wid pleasure, an' all de folks wuz mighty glad, too, 'cause dey all loved ole marster, and aldo' dey did step aroun' right peart when ole marster wuz lookin' at 'em, dyar warn' nyar han' on de place but what, ef he wanted anythin', would walk up to de back poach, an' say he warn' to see de marster.   An' ev'ybody wuz talkin' 'bout de young marster, an' de maids an' de wimmens 'bout de kitchen wuz sayin' how 'twuz de purties' chile dey ever see ; an' at dinner-time de mens (all on 'em hed holiday) come roun' de poach an' ax how de missis an' de young marster wuz, an' ole marster come out on de poach an' smile wus'n a 'possum, an' sez, ' Thankee !   Bofe doin' fust rate, boys ;' an' den he stepped back in de house, sort o' laughin' to hisse'f, an' in a minute he come out ag'in wid de baby in he arms, all wrapped up in flannens an' things, an' sez, ' Heah he is, boys.' All de folks den, dey went up on de poach to look at 'im, drappin' dey hats on de steps, an' scrapin' dey feets ez dey went up.   An' pres'n'y ole marster, lookin' down at we all chil'en all packed togedder down deah like a parecel o' sheep-burrs, cotch sight o' *me* (he knowed my name, 'cause I use' to hole he hoss fur 'im sometimes ; but he

didn' know all de chil'en by name, dey wuz so
many on 'em), an' he sez, 'Come up heah.' So up
I goes tippin', skeered like, an' old marster sez,
'Ain' you Mymie's son?' 'Yass, seh,' sez I.
'Well,' sez he, 'I'm gwine to give you to yo'
young Marse Channin' to be his body-servant,'
an' he put de baby right in my arms (it's de truth
I'm tellin' you!), an' yo' jes' ought to a-heard de
folks sayin', 'Lawd! marster, dat boy'll drap dat
chile!' 'Naw, he won't,' sez marster; 'I kin
trust 'im.' And den he sez: 'Now, Sam, from
dis time you belong to yo' young Marse Channin';
I wan' you to tek keer on 'im ez long ez he lives.
You are to be his boy from dis time. An' now,'
he sez, 'carry 'im in de house.' An' he walks
arfter me an' opens de do's fur me, an' I kyars
'im in my arms, an' lays 'im down on de bed.
An' from dat time I wuz tooken in de house to be
Marse Channin's body-servant.

"Well, you nuvver see a chile grow so.
Pres'n'y he growed up right big, an' ole marster
sez he must have some edication. So he sont 'im
to school to ole Miss Lawry down dyar, dis side o'
Cun'l Chahmb'lin's, an' I use' to go 'long wid
'im an' tote he books an' we all's snacks; an'
when he larnt to read an' spell right good, an' got
'bout so-o big, old Miss Lawry she died, an' ole
marster said he mus' have a man to teach 'im an'
trounce 'im. So we all went to Mr. Hall, whar
kep' de school-house beyant de creek, an' dyar we
went ev'y day, 'cep' Sat'd'ys of co'se, an' sich days

ez Marse Chan din' warn' go, an' ole missis begged 'im off.

"Hit wuz down dyar Marse Chan fust took notice o' Miss Anne. Mr. Hall, he taught gals ez well ez boys, an' Cun'l Chahmb'lin he sont his daughter (dat's Miss Anne I'm talkin' about). She wuz a leetle bit o' gal when she fust come. Yo' see, her ma wuz dead, an' ole Miss Lucy Chahmb'lin, she lived wid her brudder an' kep' house for 'im ; an' he wuz so busy wid politics, he didn' have much time to spyar, so he sont Miss Anne to Mr. Hall's by a 'ooman wid a note. When she come dat day in de school-house, an' all de chil'en looked at her so hard, she tu'n right red, an' tried to pull her long curls over her eyes, an' den put bofe de backs of her little han's in her two eyes, an' begin to cry to herse'f. Marse Chan he was settin' on de een' o' de bench nigh de do', an' he jes' reached out an' put he arm roun' her an' drawed her up to 'im. An' he kep' whisperin' to her, an' callin' her name, an' coddlin' her ; an' pres'n'y she took her han's down an' begin to laugh.

"Well, dey 'peared to tek' a gre't fancy to each udder from dat time. Miss Anne she warn' nuthin' but a baby hardly, an' Marse Chan he wuz a good big boy 'bout mos' thirteen years ole, I reckon. Hows'ever, dey sut'n'y wuz sot on each udder an' (yo' heah me !) ole marster an' Cun'l Chahmb'lin dey 'peared to like it 'bout well ez de chil'en. Yo' see Cun'l Chahmb'lin's place

j'ined ourn, an' it looked jes' ez natural fur dem
two chil'en to marry an' mek it one plantation,
ez it did fur de creek to run down de bottom from
our place into Cun'l Chahmb'lin's.   I don' rightly
think de chil'en thought 'bout gittin' *married*, not
den, no mo'n I thought 'bout marryin' Judy when
she wuz a little gal at Cun'l Chahmb'lin's, runnin'
'bout de house, huntin' fur Miss Lucy's spectacles ;
but dey wuz good frien's from de start.   Marse
Chan he use' to kyar Miss Anne's books fur her
ev'y day, an' ef de road wuz muddy or she wuz
tired, he use' to tote her ; an' 'twarn' hardly a day
passed dat he didn' kyar her some'n' to school—
apples or hick'y nuts, or some'n'.   He wouldn' let
none o' de chil'en tease her, nudder.   Heh !   One
day, one o' de boys poked he finger at Miss Anne,
an' arfter school Marse Chan he axed 'im 'roun'
hine de school-house out o' sight, an' ef he didn'
whop 'im !

"Marse Chan, he wuz de peartes' scholar ole
Mr. Hall hed, an' Mr. Hall he wuz mighty proud
o' 'im.   I don' think he use' to beat 'im ez much
ez he did de udders, aldo' he wuz de head in all
debilment dat went on, jes' ez he wuz in sayin' he
lessons.

"Heh ! one day in summer, jes' 'fo' de school
broke up, dyah come up a storm right sudden,
an' riz de creek (dat one yo' cross' back yonder),
an' Marse Chan he toted Miss Anne home on he
back.   He ve'y off'n did dat when de parf wuz
muddy.   But dis day when dey come to de creek,

it had done washed all de logs 'way. 'Twuz still
mighty high, so Marse Chan he put Miss Anne
down, an' he took a pole an' waded right in. Hit
took 'im long up to de shoulders. Den he waded
back, an' took Miss Anne up on his head an'
kyared her right over. At fust she wuz skeered ;
but he tol' her he could swim an' wouldn' let her
git hu't, an' den she let 'im kyar her 'cross, she
hol'in' his han's. I warn' 'long dat day, but he
sut'n'y did dat thing.

" Ole marster he wuz so pleased 'bout it, he giv'
Marse Chan a pony ; an' Marse Chan rode 'im to
school de day arfter he come, so proud, an' sayin'
how he wuz gwine to let Anne ride behine 'im ;
an' when he come home dat evenin' he wuz walkin'.
' Hi ! where's yo' pony ? ' said ole marster. ' I
give 'im to Anne,' says Marse Chan. ' She liked
'im, an'—I kin walk.' ' Yes,' sez ole marster,
laughin', ' I s'pose you's already done giv' her
yo'se'f, an' nex' thing I know you'll be givin' her
this plantation and all my niggers.'

" Well, about a fortnight or sich a matter arfter
dat, Cun'l Chahmb'lin sont over an' invited all o'
we all over to dinner, an' Marse Chan wuz 'spressly
named in de note whar Ned brought ; an' arfter
dinner he made ole Phil, whar wuz his ker'ige-
driver, bring roun' Marse Chan's pony wid a little
side-saddle on 'im, an' a beautiful little hoss wid a
bran'-new saddle an' bridle on 'im ; an' he gits
up an' meks Marse Chan a gre't speech, an' pre-
sents 'im de little hoss ; an' den he calls Miss

Anne, an' she comes out on de poach in a little
ridin' frock, an' dey puts her on her pony, an'
Marse Chan mounts his hoss, an' dey goes to ride,
while de grown folks is a-laughin' an' chattin' an'
smokin' dey cigars.

"Dem wuz good ole times, marster—de bes'
Sam ever see! Dey wuz, in fac'! Niggers didn'
hed nothin' 't all to do—jes' hed to 'ten' to de
feedin', an' cleanin' de hosses, an' doin' what de
marster tell 'em to do; an' when dey wuz sick,
dey had things sont 'em out de house, an' de same
doctor come to see 'em whar 'ten' to de white folks
when dey wuz po'ly. Dyar warn' no trouble nor
nothin'.

"Well, things tuk a change arfter dat. Marse
Chan he went to de bo'din' school, whar he use' to
write to me constant. Ole missis use' to read me
de letters, an' den I'd git Miss Anne to read 'em
ag'in to me when I'd see her. He use' to write to
her too, an' she use' to write to him too. Den
Miss Anne she wuz sont off to school too. An' in
de summer time dey'd bofe come home, an' yo'
hardly knowed whether Marse Chan lived at home
or over at Cun'l Chahmb'lin's. He wuz over
dyah constant. 'Twuz always ridin' or fishin'
down dyah, in de river; or sometimes he' go over
dyah, an' 'im an' she'd go out an' set in de yard
onder de trees; she settin' up mekin' out she wuz
knittin' some sort o' bright-cullored some'n', wid
de grarss growin' all up 'g'inst her, an' her hat
th'owed back on her neck, an' he readin' to her

out books ; an' sometimes dey'd bofe read out de same book, fust one an' den todder. I use' to see 'em ! Dat wuz when dey wuz growin' up like.

"Den ole marster he run for Congress, an' ole Cun'l Chahmb'lin he wuz put up to run 'g'inst ole marster by de Dimicrats ; but ole marster he beat 'im. Yo' know he wuz gwine do dat ! Co'se he wuz ! Dat made ole Cun'l Chahmb'lin mighty mad, and dey stopt visitin' each udder reg'lar, like dey had been doin' all 'long. Den Cun'l Chahmb'lin he sort o' got in debt, an' sell some o' he niggers, an' dat's de way de fuss begun. Dat's whar de lawsuit cum from. Ole marster he didn' like nobody to sell niggers, an' knowin' dat Cun'l Chahmb'lin wuz sellin' o' his, he writ an' offered to buy his M'ria an' all her chil'en, 'cause she hed married our Zeek'yel. An' don' yo' t'ink, Cun'l Chahmb'lin axed ole marster mo' 'n th'ee niggers wuz wuth fur M'ria. Befo' old marster bought her, dough, de sheriff cum an' levelled on M'ria an' a whole parcel o' udder niggers. Ole marster he went to de sale, an' bid for 'em ; but Cun'l Chahmb'lin he got some one to bid 'g'inst ole marster. Dey wuz knocked out to ole marster dough, an' den dey hed a big lawsuit, an' ole marster wuz agwine to co't, off an' on, fur some years, till at lars' de co't decided dat M'ria belonged to ole marster. Ole Cun'l Chahmb'lin den wuz so mad he sued ole marster for a little strip o' lan' down dyah on de line fence, whar he said belonged to 'im. Evy'body knowed hit belonged to ole marster. Ef yo' go down dyah now, I kin show it to yo', inside de line fence, whar it hed done bin ever since long befo' ole marster wuz born. But Cun'l Chahmb'lin wuz a mons'us perseverin' man, an' ole marster he wouldn' let nobody run over 'im. No, dat he wouldn'! So dey wuz agwine down to co't about dat, fur I don' know how long, till ole marster beat 'im.

"All dis time, yo' know, Marse Chan wuz agoin' back'ads an' for'ads to college, an' wuz growed up a ve'y fine young man. He wuz a ve'y likely gent'man! Miss Anne she hed done mos' growed up, too—wuz puttin' her hyar up like ole missis use' to put hers up, an' 't wuz jes' ez bright ez de sorrel's mane when de sun cotch on it, an' her eyes wuz gre't big dark eyes, like her pa's, on'y bigger an' not so fierce, an' 'twarn' none o' de young ladies ez purty ez she wuz. She an' Marse Chan still set a heap o' sto' by one 'nudder, but I don' t'ink dey wuz easy wid each udder ez when he used to tote her home from school on his back. Marse Chan he use' to love de ve'y groun' she walked on, dough, in my 'pinion. Heh! His face 'twould light up whenever she come into chu'ch, or anywhere, jes' like de sun hed come th'oo a chink on it suddenly.

"Den ole marster lost he eyes. D' yo' ever hyah 'bout dat? Heish! Didn' yo'? Well, one night de big barn cotch fire. De stables, yo' know, wuz under de big barn, an' all de hosses wuz in dyah. Hit 'peared to me like 'twarn' no time befo' all de folks an' de neighbors dey come, an' dey wuz a-totin' water, an' a-tryin' to save de po' critters, an' dey got a heap on 'em out ; but de ker'ige-hosses dey wouldn' come out, an' dey wuz a-runnin' back'ads an' for'ads inside de stalls, a-nikerin' an' a-screamin', like dey knowed dey time hed come. Yo' could heah 'em so pitiful, an' pres'n'y ole marster said to Ham Fisher (he wuz de ker'ige-driver), ' Go in dyah an' try to save 'em ; don' let 'em bu'n to death.' An' Ham he went right in. An' jes' arfter he got in, de shed whar it hed fus' cotch fell in, an' de sparks shot 'way up in de air ; an' Ham didn' come back, an' de fire begun to lick out under de eaves over whar de ker'ige hosses' stalls wuz, an' all of a sudden ole marster tu'ned and kissed ole missis, who wuz standin' nigh him, wid her face jes' ez white ez a sperit's, an', befo' anybody knowed what he wuz gwine do, jumped right in de do', an' de smoke come po'in' out behine 'im. Well, seh, I nuvver 'specks to hyah tell Judgment sich a soun' ez de folks set up. Ole missis she jes' drapt down on her knees in de mud an' prayed out loud. Hit 'peared like her pra'r wuz heard ; for in a minit, right out de same do', kyarin' Ham Fisher in his arms, come ole marster, wid his clo'es all blazin'. Dey flung water on 'im, an' put 'im out ; an', ef you b'lieve me, yo' wouldn' a-knowed 'twuz ole marster. Yo' see, he hed find Ham Fisher done fall down in de smoke right by de ker'ige-hoss' stalls, whar he sont him, an' he hed to tote 'im

back in his arms th'oo de fire what hed done cotch
de front part o' de stable, an' to keep de flame
from gittin' down Ham Fisher's th'ote he hed tuk
off his own hat and mashed it all over Ham Fisher's
face, an' he hed kep' Ham Fisher from bein' so
much bu'nt ; but *he* wuz bu'nt dreadful ! His
beard an' hyar wuz all nyawed off, an' his face an'
han's an' neck wuz scorified terrible.   Well, he jes'
laid Ham Fisher down, an' then he kind o' stag-
gered for'ad, an' ole missis ketch' 'im in her
arms.   Ham Fisher, he warnt bu'nt so bad, an'
he got out in a month or two ; an' arfter a long
time, ole marster he got well, too ; but he wuz
always stone bline arfter dat.   He nuvver could
see none from dat night.

"Marse Chan he comed home from college
toreckly, an' he sut'n'y did nuss ole marster
faithful—jes' like a 'ooman.   Den he took charge
o' de plantation arfter dat ; an' I use' to wait on
'im jes' like when we wuz boys togedder ; an'
sometimes we'd slip off an' have a fox-hunt, an'
he'd be jes' like he wuz in ole times, befo' ole
marster got bline, an' Miss Anne Chahmb'lin stopt
comin' over to our house, an' settin' onder de
trees, readin' out de same book.

"He sut'n'y wuz good to me.   Nothin' nuvver
made no diffunce 'bout dat.   He nuvver hit me a
lick in his life—an' nuvver let nobody else do it,
nudder.

"I 'members one day, when he wuz a leetle bit
o' boy, ole marster hed done tole we all chil'en not

to slide on de straw-stacks ; an' one day me an'
Marse Chan thought ole marster hed done gone
'way from home. We watched him git on he
hoss an' ride up de road out o' sight, an' we wuz
out in de field a-slidin' an' a-slidin', when up comes
ole marster. We started to run ; but he hed done
see us, an' he called us to come back ; an' sich a
whoppin' ez he did gi' us !

"Fust he took Marse Chan, an' den he teched
me up. He nuvver hu't me, but in co'se I wuz
a-hollerin' ez hard ez I could stave it, 'cause I
knowed dat wuz gwine mek him stop. Marse Chan
he hed'n open he mouf long ez ole marster wuz
tunin' 'im ; but soon ez he commence warmin' me
an' I begin to holler, Marse Chan he bu'st out
cryin', an' stept right in befo' ole marster, an'
ketchin' de whop, sed :

"'Stop, seh ! Yo' sha'n't whop 'im ; he
b'longs to me, an' ef you hit 'im another lick I'll
set 'im free !'

"I wish yo' hed see ole marster. Marse Chan
he warn' mo'n eight years ole, an' dyah dey wuz—
ole marster stan'in' wid he whop raised up, an'
Marse Chan red an' cryin', hol'in' on to it, an'
sayin' I b'longst to 'im.

"Ole marster, he raise' de whop, an' den he
drapt it, an' broke out in a smile over he face, an'
he chuck' Marse Chan onder der chin, an' tu'n
right roun' an' went away, laughin' to hisse'f, an'
I heah' 'im tellin' ole missis dat evenin', an' laughin' 'bout it.

"'Twan' so mighty long arfter dat when dey fust got to talkin' 'bout de war. Dey wuz a-dictatin' back'ads an' for'ads 'bout it fur two or th'ee years 'fo' it come sho' nuff, you know. Ole marster, he wuz a Whig, an' of co'se Marse Chan he tuk after he pa. Cun'l Chahmb'lin, he wuz a Dimicrat. He wuz in favor of de war, an' ole marster and Marse Chan dey wuz agin' it. Dey wuz a-talkin' 'bout it all de time, an' purty soon Cun'l Chahmb'lin he went about ev'vywhar speakin' an' noratin' 'bout Ferginia ought to secede ; an' Marse Chan he wuz picked up to talk agin' 'im. Dat wuz de way dey come to fight de duil. I sut'n'y wuz skeered fur Marse Chan dat mawnin', an' he was jes' ez cool ! Yo' see, it happen so : Marse Chan he wuz a-speakin' down at de Deep Creek Tavern, an' he kind o' got de bes' of ole Cun'l Chahmb'lin. All de white folks laughed an' hoorawed, an' ole Cun'l Chahmb'lin—my Lawd ! I t'ought he'd 'a' bu'st, he wuz so mad. Well, when it come to his time to speak, he jes' light into Marse Chan. He call 'im a traitor, an' a ab'litionis', an' I don' know what all. Marse Chan, he jes' kep' cool till de ole Cun'l light into he pa. Ez soon ez he name ole marster, I seen Marse Chan sort o' lif' up he head. D' yo' ever see a hoss rar he head up right sudden at night when he see somethin' comin' to'ds 'im from de side an' he don' know what 'tis ? Ole Cun'l Chahmb'lin, he went right on. He said ole marster hed taught Marse Chan ; dat ole marster wuz a wuss ab'litionis' dan he son. I looked at Marse Chan, an' sez to myse'f : ' Fo' Gord ! old Cun'l Chahmb'lin better min', an' I hedn' got de wuds out, when ole Cun'l Chahmb'lin 'cuse' ole marster o' cheatin' 'im out o' he niggers, an' stealin' piece o' he lan'—dat's de lan' I tole you 'bout. Well, seh, nex' thing I knowed, I heahed Marse Chan—hit all happen right 'long togedder, like lightnin' an' thunder when dey hit right at you—I heah 'im say :

" Cun'l Chahmb'lin, what you say is false, an' yo' know it to be so. You have wilfully slandered one of the pures' an' nobles' men Gord ever made, an' nothin' but yo' gray hyars protects you.'

" Well, ole Cun'l Chahmb'lin, he ra'ed an' he pitch'd. He said he wan' too ole, an' he'd show 'im so.

" ' Ve'y well,' says Marse Chan.

" De meetin' broke up den. I wuz hol'in de hosses out dyar in de road by de een' o' de poach, an' I see Marse Chan talkin' an' talkin' to Mr. Gordon an' anudder gent'man, an' den he come out an' got on de sorrel an' galloped off. Soon ez he got out o' sight, he pulled up, an' we walked along tell we come to de road whar leads off to'ds Mr. Barbour's. He wuz de big lawyer o' de country. Dar he tu'ned off. All dis time he hedn' sed a wud, 'cep' to kind o' mumble to hisse'f now an' den. When we got to Mr. Barbour's, he got down an' went in. Dat wuz in de late winter ; de folks wuz jes' beginnin' to plough fur corn. He stayed dyar 'bout two hours, an' when he come out

Mr. Barbour come out to de gate wid 'im an' shake han's arfter he got up in de saddle. Den we all rode off. 'Twuz late den—good dark ; an' we rid ez hard ez we could, tell we come to de ole school-house at ole Cun'l Chahmb'lin's gate. When we got dar Marse Chan got down an' walked right slow 'roun' de house. Arfter lookin' 'roun' a little while an' tryin' de do' to see ef it wuz shet, he walked down de road tell he got to de creek. He stop' dyar a little while an' picked up two or three little rocks an' frowed 'em in, an' pres'n'y he got up an' we come on home. Ez he got down, he tu'ned to me an', rubbin' de sorrel's nose, said : ' Have 'em well fed, Sam ; I'll want 'em early in de mawnin'.'

"Dat night at supper he laugh an' talk, an' he set at de table a long time. Arfter ole marster went to bed, he went in de charmber an' set on de bed by 'im talkin' to 'im an' tellin' 'im 'bout de meetin' an' ev'ything ; but he never mention ole Cun'l Chahmb'lin's name. When he got up to come out to de office in de yard, whar he slept, he stooped down an' kissed 'im jes' like he wuz a baby layin' dyar in de bed, an' he'd hardly let ole missis go at all. I knowed some'n wuz up, an' nex' mawnin' I called 'im early befo' light, like he tole me, an' he dressed an' come out pres'n'y jes' like he wuz goin' to chu'ch. I had de hosses ready, an' we went out de back way to'ds de river. Ez we rode along, he said :

"'Sam, you an' I wuz boys togedder, wa'n't we?'

" ' Yes,' sez I, ' Marse Chan, dat we wuz.'

" ' You have been ve'y faithful to me,' sez he, ' an' I have seen to it that you are well provided fur. You wan' to marry Judy, I know, an' you'll be able to buy her ef you want to.'

" Den he tole me he wuz goin' to fight a duil, an' in case he should git shot, he had set me free an' giv' me nuff to tek keer o' me an' my wife ez long ez we lived. He said he'd like me to stay an' tek keer o' ole marster an' ole missis ez long ez dey lived, an' he said it wouldn' be very long, he reckoned. Dat wuz de on'y time he voice broke— when he said dat ; an' I couldn' speak a wud, my th'oat choked me so.

" When we come to de river, we tu'ned right up de bank, an' arfter ridin' 'bout a mile or sich a matter, we stopped whar dey wuz a little clearin' wid elder bushes on one side an' two big gum trees on de udder, an' de sky wuz all red, an' de water down to'ds whar de sun wuz comin' wuz jes' like de sky.

" Pres'n'y Mr. Gordon he come wid a 'hogany box 'bout so big 'fore 'im, an' he got down, an' Marse Chan tole me to tek all de hosses an' go 'roun' behine de bushes whar I tell you 'bout— off to one side ; an' 'fore I got 'roun' dar, ole Cun'l Chahmb'lin an' Mr. Hennin an' Dr. Call come ridin' from tudder way, to'ds ole Cun'l Chahmb'lin's. When dey hed tied dey hosses, de udder gent'mens went up to whar Mr. Gordon wuz, an' arfter some chattin' Mr. Hennin step' off 'bout fur ez 'cross dis road, or mebbe it mout be a

little furder ; an' den I seed 'em th'oo de bushes
loadin' de pistils, an' talk' a little while ; an' den
Marse Chan an' ole Cun'l Chahmb'lin walked up
wid de pistils in dey han's, an' Marse Chan he
stood wid his face right to'ds de sun. I seen it
shine on 'im jes' ez it come up over de low groun's,
an' he look' like he did sometimes when he come
out of chu'ch. I wuz so skeered I couldn' say
nuthin'. Ole Cun'l Chahmb'lin could shoot fust
rate, an' Marse Chan he never missed.

"Den I heared Mr. Gordon say, 'Gent'mens, is
yo' ready ?' and bofe of 'em sez, 'Ready,' jes' so.

"An' he sez, 'Fire, one, two'—an' ez he said
'one,' ole Cun'l Chahmb'lin raised he pistil an'
shot right at Marse Chan. De ball went th'oo his
hat. I seen he hat sort o' settle on he head ez de
bullit hit it, an' *he* jes' tilted his pistil up in de a'r
an' shot—*bang ;* an' ez de pistil went *bang,* he sez
to Cun'l Chahmb'lin, 'I mek you a present to yo'
fam'ly, seh !'

"Well, dey had some talkin' arfter dat. I
didn' git rightly what it wuz ; but it 'peared like
Cun'l Chahmb'lin he warn't satisfied, an' wanted
to have anudder shot. De seconds dey wuz talkin', an' pres'n'y dey put de pistils up, an' Marse
Chan an' Mr. Gordon shook han's wid Mr. Hennin
an' Dr. Call, an' come an' got on dey hosses. An'
Cun'l Chahmb'lin he got on his horse an' rode
away wid de udder gent'mens, lookin' like he
did de day befo' when all de people laughed at
'im.

" I b'lieve ole Cun'l Chahmb'lin wan' to shoot Marse Chan, anyway !

" We come on home to breakfast, I totin' de box wid de pistils befo' me on the roan. Would you b'lieve me, seh, Marse Chan he nuvver said a wud 'bout it to ole marster or nobody. Ole missis didn' fin' out 'bout it for mo'n a month, an' den, Lawd ! how she did cry and kiss Marse Chan ; an' ole marster, aldo' he never say much, he wuz jes' ez please' ez ole missis. He call' me in de room an' made me tole 'im all 'bout it, an' when I got th'oo he gi' me five dollars an' a pyar of breeches.

" But ole Cun'l Chahmb'lin he nuvver did furgive Marse Chan, and Miss Anne she got mad too. Wimmens is mons'us onreasonable nohow. Dey's jes' like a catfish : you can n' tek' hole on 'em like udder folks, an' when you gits 'm yo' can n' always hole 'em.

" What meks me think so ? Heaps o' things— dis : Marse Chan he done gi' Miss Anne her pa jes' ez good ez I gi' Marse Chan's dawg sweet 'taters, an' she git mad wid 'im ez if he hed kill 'im 'stid o' sen'in' 'im back to her dat mawnin' whole an' soun'. B'lieve me ! she wouldn' even speak to 'im arfter dat !

" Don' I 'member dat mawnin'!

" We wuz gwine fox-huntin', 'bout six weeks or sich a matter arfter de duil, an' we met Miss Anne ridin' 'long wid anudder lady an' two gent'mens whar wuz stayin' at her house. Dyar wuz always

some one or nudder dyar co'ting her. Well, dat
mawnin' we meet 'em right in de road. 'Twuz de
fust time Marse Chan had see her sence de duil,
an' he raises he hat ez he pahss, an' she looks right
at 'im wid her head up in de yair like she nuvver
see 'im befo' in her born days; an' when she
comes by me, she sez, 'Good-mawnin', Sam!'
Gord! I nuvver see nuthin' like de look dat
come on Marse Chan's face when she pahss 'im like
dat. He gi' de sorrel a pull dat fotch 'im back
settin' down in de san' on he hanches. He ve'y
lips wuz white. I tried to keep up wid 'im, but
'twarn' no use. He sont me back home pres'n'y,
an' he rid on. I sez to myself, 'Cun'l Chahm-
b'lin, don' yo' meet Marse Chan dis mawnin'.
He ain' bin lookin' 'roun' de ole school-house, whar
he an' Miss Anne use' to go to school to ole Mr.
Hall together, fur nuffin'. He won' stan' no prodjickin' to-day.'

" He nuvver come home dat night tell 'way late,
an' ef he'd been fox-huntin' it mus' ha' been de ole
red whar lives down in de greenscum mashes he'd
been chasin'. De way de sorrel wuz gormed up wid
sweat an' mire sut'n'y did hu't me. He walked
up to de stable wid he head down all de way, an'
I'se seen 'im go eighty miles of a winter day, an'
prance into de stable at night ez fresh ez ef he hed
jes' cantered over to ole Cun'l Chahmb'lin's to
supper. I nuvver seen a hoss beat so sence I
knowed de fetlock from de fo'lock, an' bad ez he
wuz he wan' ez bad ez Marse Chan.

" Whew ! he didn' git over dat thing, seh—he nuvver did git over it.

" De war come on jes' den, an' Marse Chan wuz elected cap'n ; but he wouldn' tek it. He said Firginia hadn' seceded, an' he wuz gwine stan' by her. Den dey 'lected Mr. Gordon cap'n.

" I sut'n'y did wan' Marse Chan to tek de place, cuz I knowed he wuz gwine tek me wid 'im. He wan' gwine widout Sam. An' beside, he look so po' an' thin, I thought he wuz gwine die.

" Of co'se ole missis she heard 'bout it, an' she met Miss Anne in de road, an' cut her jes' like Miss Anne cut Marse Chan.

" Ole missis, she wuz proud ez anybody ! So we wuz mo' strangers dan ef we hadn' live' in a hunderd miles of each udder. An' Marse Chan he wuz gittin' thinner an' thinner, an' Firginia she come out, an' den Marse Chan he went to Richmond an' listed, an' come back an' sey he wuz a private, an' he didn' know whe'r he could tek me or not. He writ to Mr. Gordon, hows'ever, and 'twuz decided that when he went I wuz to go 'long an' wait on him, an' de cap'n too. I didn' min' dat, yo' know, long ez I could go wid Marse Chan, an' I like' Mr. Gordon, anyways.

" Well, one night Marse Chan come back from de offis wid a telegram dat say, ' Come at once,' so he wuz to start nex' mawnin'. He uniform wuz all ready, gray wid yaller trimmin's, an' mine wuz ready too, an' he had ole marster's sword, whar de State gi' 'im in de Mexikin war ; an' he trunks

wuz all packed wid ev'rything in 'em, an' my chist
wuz packed too, an' Jim Rasher he druv 'em over
to de depo' in de waggin, an' we wuz to start nex'
mawnin' 'bout light. Dis wuz 'bout de las' o'
spring, you know. Dat night ole missis made
Marse Chan dress up in he uniform, an' he sut'n'y
did look splendid wid he long mustache an' he
wavin' hyar and he tall figger.

"Arfter supper he come down an' sez : ' Sam, I
wan' you to tek dis note an' kyar it over to Cun'l
Chahmb'lin's, an' gi' it to Miss Anne wid yo' own
han's, an' bring me wud what she sez. Don' let
any one know 'bout it, or know why you've gone.'
' Yes, seh,' sez I.

"Yo' see, I knowed Miss Anne's maid over at
ole Cun'l Chahmb'lin's—dat wuz Judy whar is
my wife now—an' I knowed I could wuk it. So I
tuk de roan an' rid over, an' tied 'im down de hill
in de cedars, an' I wen' 'roun' to de back yard.
'Twuz a right blowy sort o' night ; de moon wuz jes'
risin', but de clouds wuz so big it didn' shine 'cep'
th'oo a crack now an' den. I soon foun' my gal,
an' arfter tellin' her two or three lies 'bout herse'f,
I got her to go in an' ax Miss Anne to come to de
do'. When she come, I gi' her de note, an' arfter
a little while she bro't me anudder, an' I tole her
good-by, an' she gi' me a dollar, an' I come home
an' gi' de letter to Marse Chan. He read it, an'
tole me to have de hosses ready at twenty minits
to twelve at de corner of de garden. An' jes'
befo' dat he come out ez ef he wuz gwine to bed,

but instid he come, an' we all struck out to'ds Cun'l Chahmb'lin's. When we got mos' to de gate, de hosses got sort o' skeered, an' I see dey wuz some'n or somebody standin' jes' inside; an' Marse Chan he jumpt off de sorrel an' flung me de bridle and he walked up.

"She spoke fust ('twuz Miss Anne had done come out dyar to meet Marse Chan), an' she sez, jes' ez cold ez a chill, 'Well, seh, I granted your favor. I wished to relieve myse'f of de obligations you placed me under a few months ago, when you made me a present of my father, whom you fust insulted an' then prevented from gittin' satisfaction.'

"Marse Chan he didn' speak fur a minit, an' den he said : 'Who is with you ?' (Dat wuz ev'y wud.)

"'No one,' sez she; 'I came alone.'

"'My God!' sez he, 'you didn' come all through those woods by yourse'f at this time o' night?'

"'Yes, I'm not afraid,' sez she. (An' heah dis nigger ! I don' b'lieve she wuz.)

" De moon come out, an' I cotch sight o' her stan'in' dyar in her white dress, wid de cloak she had wrapped herse'f up in drapped off on de groun', an' she didn' look like she wuz 'feared o' nuthin'. She wuz mons'us purty ez she stood dyar wid de green bushes behine her, an' she hed jes' a few flowers in her breas'—right hyah—and some leaves in her sorrel hyar; an' de moon come out an' shined down on her hyar an' her frock, an' 'peared like

de light wuz jes' stan'in' off it ez she stood dyar
lookin' at Marse Chan wid her head tho'd back, jes'
like dat mawnin' when she pahss Marse Chan in
de road widout speakin' to 'im, an' sez to me,
'Good mawnin', Sam.'

"Marse Chan, he den tole her he hed come to
say good-by to her, ez he wuz gwine 'way to de
war nex' mawnin'.   I wuz watchin' on her, an'
I tho't when Marse Chan tole her dat, she sort o'
started an' looked up at 'im like she wuz mighty
sorry, an' 'peared like she didn' stan' quite so
straight arfter dat.   Den Marse Chan he went on
talkin' right fars' to her ; an' he tole her how he
had loved her ever sence she wuz a little bit o'
baby mos', an' how he nuvver 'membered de time
when he hedn' 'spected to marry her.   He tole
her it wuz his love for her dat hed made 'im stan'
fust at school an' collige, an' hed kep' 'im good
an' pure ; an' now he wuz gwine 'way, wouldn'
she let it be like 'twuz in ole times, an' ef he
come back from de war wouldn' she try to t'ink
on him ez she use' to do when she wuz a little
guirl ?

"Marse Chan he had done been talkin' so
serious, he hed done tuk Miss Anne's han', an'
wuz lookin' down in her face like he wuz list'nin'
wid his eyes.

"Arfter a minit Miss Anne she said somethin',
an' Marse Chan he cotch her udder han' an' sez :

"'But if you love me, Anne ?'

"When he sed dat, she tu'ned her head 'way

from 'im, an' wait' a minit, an' den she sed—right clear :

" ' But I don' love yo'.' (Jes' dem th'ee wuds !) De wuds fall right slow—like dirt falls out a spade on a coffin when yo's buryin' anybody an' seys, ' Uth to uth.' Marse Chan he jes' let her hand drap, an' he stiddy hisse'f 'g'inst de gate-pos', an' he didn' speak torekly. When he did speak, all he sez wuz :

" ' I mus' see you home safe.'

" I 'clar, marster, I didn' know 'twuz Marse Chan's voice tell I look at 'im right good. Well, she wouldn' let 'im go wid her. She jes' wrap' her cloak 'roun' her shoulders, an' wen' 'long back by herse'f, widout doin' more'n jes' look up once at Marse Chan leanin' dyah 'g'inst de gate-pos' in he sodger clo'es, wid he eyes on de groun'. She said ' Good-by ' sort o' sorf, an' Marse Chan, widout lookin' up, shake han's wid her, an' she wuz done gone down de road. Soon ez she got 'mos' 'roun' de curve, Marse Chan he followed her, keepin' under de trees so ez not to be seen, an' I led de hosses on down de road behine 'im. He kep' 'long behine her tell she wuz safe in de house, an' den he come an' got on he hoss, an' we all come home.

" Nex' mawnin' we all come off to j'ine de army. An' dey wuz a-drillin' an' a-drillin' all 'bout for a while an' dey went 'long wid all de res' o' de army, an' I went wid Marse Chan an' clean he boots, an' look arfter de tent, an' tek keer o' him an' de hosses. An' Marse Chan, he wan' a bit like he use' to be. He wuz so solum an' moanful all de time, at leas' 'cep' when dyah wuz gwine to be a fight. Den he'd peartin' up, an' he alwuz rode at de head o' de company 'cause he wuz tall; an' hit wan' on'y in battles whar all his company wuz dat *he* went, but he use' to volunteer whenever de cun'l wanted anybody to fine out anythin', an' 'twuz so dangersome he didn' like to mek one man go no sooner'n anudder, yo' know, an' ax'd who'd volunteer. *He* 'peared to like to go prowlin' aroun' 'mong dem Yankees, an' he use' to tek me wid 'im whenever he could. Yes, seh, he sut'n'y wuz a good sodger! He didn' mine bullets no more'n he did so many draps o' rain. But I use' to be pow'ful skeered sometimes. It jes' use' to 'pear like fun to 'im. In camp he use' to be so sorrerful he'd hardly open he mouf. You'd 'a' tho't he wuz seekin', he used to look so moanful; but jes' le' 'im git into danger, an' he use' to be like ole times—jolly an' laughin' like when he wuz a boy.

"When Cap'n Gordon got he leg shot off, dey mek Marse Chan cap'n on de spot, 'cause one o' de lieutenants got kilt de same day, an' tor'er one (named Mr. Ronny) wan' no 'count, an' all de company sed Marse Chan wuz de man.

"An' Marse Chan he wuz jes' de same. He didn' never mention Miss Anne's name, but I knowed he wuz thinkin' on her constant. One night he wuz settin' by de fire in camp, an' Mr.

Ronny—he wuz de secon' lieutenant—got to talk-in' 'bout ladies, an' he say all sorts o' things 'bout 'em, an' I see Marse Chan kinder lookin' mad ; an' de lieutenant mention Miss Anne's name. He hed been courtin' Miss Anne 'bout de time Marse Chan fit de duil wid her pa, an' Miss Anne hed kicked 'im, dough he wuz mighty rich, 'cause he warn' nuthin' but a half-strainer, an' 'cause she like Marse Chan, I believe, dough she didn' speak to 'im ; an' Mr. Ronny he got drunk, an' 'cause Cun'l Chahmb'lin tole 'im not to come dyah no more, he got mighty mad. An' dat evenin' I'se tellin' yo' 'bout, he wuz talkin', an' he mention' Miss Anne's name. I see Marse Chan tu'n he eye 'roun' on 'im an' keep it on he face, an' pres'n'y Mr. Ronny said he wuz gwine hev some fun dyah yit. He didn' mention her name dat time ; but he said dey wuz all on 'em a parecel of stuck-up 'risticrats, an' her pa wan' no gent'man anyway, and *she*—— I don' know what he wuz gwine say (he nuvver said it), fur ez he got dat far Marse Chan riz up an' hit 'im a crack, an' he fall like he hed been hit wid a fence-rail. He challenged Marse Chan to fight a duil, an' Marse Chan he excepted de chal-lenge, an' dey wuz gwine fight ; but some on 'em tole 'im Marse Chan wan' gwine mek a present o' him to his fam'ly, an' he got somebody to bre'k up de duil ; 'twan' nuthin' dough, but he wuz 'fred to fight Marse Chan. An' purty soon he lef' de comp'ny.

"Well, I got one o' de gent'mens to write Judy

a letter for me, an' I tole her all 'bout de fight, an'
how Marse Chan knock Mr. Ronny over fur speakin' discontemptuous o' Cun'l Chahmb'lin, an' I
tole her how Marse Chan wuz a-dyin' fur love o'
Miss Anne. An' Judy she gits Miss Anne to read
de letter fur her. Den Miss Anne she tells her pa,
an'—you mind, Judy tells me all dis arfterwards,
an' she say when Cun'l Chahmb'lin hear 'bout it,
he wuz settin' on de poach, an' he set still a good
while, an' den he sey to hisse'f :

"' Well, he carn' he'p bein' a Whig.'

" An' den he gits up an' walks up to Miss Anne
an' looks at her right hard ; an' Miss Anne she
hed done tu'n away her head an' wuz makin' out
she wuz fixin' a rose-bush 'g'inst de poach ; an'
when her pa kep' lookin' at her, her face got jes'
de color o' de roses on de bush, an' pres'n'y her
pa sez :

"' Anne ! '

" An' she tu'ned 'roun', an' he sez :

"' Do yo' want 'im ?'

" An' she sez, ' Yes,' an' put her head on he
shoulder an' begin to cry ; an' he sez :

"' Well, I won' stan' between yo' no longer.
Write to 'im an' say so.'

" We didn' know nuthin' 'bout dis den. We
wuz a-fightin' an' a-fightin' all dat time ; an' come
one day a letter to Marse Chan, an' I see 'im start
to read it in his tent, an' he face hit look so cu'ious,
an' he han's trembled so I couldn' mek out what
wuz de matter wid 'im. An' he fold' de letter up

an' wen' out an' wen' 'way down 'hine de camp,
an' stayed dyah 'bout nigh an hour. Well, seh, I
wuz on de lookout for 'im when he come back, an',
fo' Gord, ef he face didn' shine like a angel's. I
say to myse'f, ' Um'm ! ef de glory o' Gord ain'
done shine on 'im ! ' An' what yo' 'spose 'twuz ?

" He tuk me wid 'im dat evenin', an' he tell me
he hed done git a letter from Miss Anne, an' Marse
Chan he eyes look like gre't big stars, an' he face
wuz jes' like 'twuz dat mawnin' when de sun riz up
over de low groun's, an' I see 'im stan'in' dyah
wid de pistil in he han', lookin' at it, an' not
knowin' but what it mout be de lars' time, an' he
done mek up he mine not to shoot ole Cun'l
Chahmb'lin fur Miss Anne's sake, what writ 'im
de letter.

" He fold' de letter wha' was in his han' up, an'
put it in he inside pocket—right dyar on de lef'
side ; an' den he tole me he tho't mebbe we wuz
gwine hev some warm wuk in de nex' two or
th'ee days, an arfter dat ef Gord speared 'im he'd
git a leave o' absence fur a few days, an' we'd go
home.

" Well, dat night de orders come, an' we all hed
to git over to'ds Romney ; an' we rid all night till
'bout light ; an' we halted right on a little creek,
an' we stayed dyah till mos' breakfas' time, an' I see
Marse Chan set down on de groun' 'hine a bush
an' read dat letter over an' over. I watch 'im, an'
de battle wuz a-goin' on, but we hed orders to stay
'hine de hill, an' ev'y now an' den de bullets

would cut de limbs o' de trees right over us, an'
one o' dem big shells what goes '*Awhar—awhar—
awhar!*' would fall right 'mong us; but Marse
Chan he didn' mine it no mo'n nuthin'! Den it
'peared to git closer an' thicker, an' Marse Chan
he calls me, an' I crep' up, an' he sez:

"'Sam, we'se goin' to win in dis battle, an'
den we'll go home an' git married; an' I'se goin'
home wid a star on my collar.' An' den he sez,
'Ef I'm wounded, kyar me home, yo' hear?' An'
I sez, 'Yes, Marse Chan.'

"Well, jes' den dey blowed boots an' saddles
an' we mounted; an' de orders come to ride 'roun'
de slope, an' Marse Chan's company wuz de secon';
an' when we got 'roun' dyah, we wuz right in it.
Hit wuz de wust place ever dis nigger got in. An'
dey said, 'Charge 'em!' an' my king! ef ever you
see bullets fly, dey did dat day. Hit wuz jes' like
hail; an' we wen' down de slope (I long wid de
res') an' up de hill right to'ds de cannons, an' de
fire wuz so strong dyar (dey hed a whole rigiment
o' infintrys layin' down dyar onder de cannons) our
lines sort o' broke an' stop; de cun'l was kilt, an'
I b'lieve dey wuz jes' 'bout to bre'k all to pieces,
when Marse Chan rid up an' cotch hol' de fleg an'
hollers, 'Foller me!' an' rid strainin' up de hill
'mong de cannons. I seen 'im when he went, de
sorrel four good lengths ahead o' ev'y udder hoss,
jes' like he use' to be in a fox-hunt, an' de whole
rigiment right arfter 'im. Yo' ain' nuvver hear
thunder! Fust thing I knowed, de roan roll' head

over heels an' flung me up 'g'inst de bank, like yo'
chuck a nubbin over 'g'inst de foot o' de corn pile.
An' dat's what kep' me from bein' kilt, I 'specks.
Judy she say she think 'twuz Providence, but I
think 'twuz de bank. Of co'se, Providence put de
bank dyar, but how come Providence nuvver saved
Marse Chan! When I look' 'roun', de roan wuz
layin' dyah by me, stone dead, wid a cannon-ball
gone 'mos' th'oo him, an' our men hed done swep'
dem on t'udder side from de top o' de hill. 'Twan'
mo'n a minit, de sorrel come gallupin' back wid
his mane flyin', an' de rein hangin' down on one
side to his knee. ' Dyar !' says I, ' fo' Gord ! I
'specks dey done kill Marse Chan, an' I promised
to tek care on him.'

" I jumped up an' run over de bank, an' dyar
wid a whole lot o' dead men, an' some not dead
yit, onder one o' de guns wid de fleg still in he
han', an' a bullet right th'oo he body, lay Marse
Chan. I tu'n' 'im over an' call 'im ' Marse Chan !'
but 'twan' no use, he wuz done gone home, sho'
'nuff. I pick' 'im up in my arms wid de fleg still
in he han's, an' toted 'im back jes' like I did dat
day when he wuz a baby, an' ole marster gin 'im
to me in my arms, an' sez he could trus' me, an'
tell me to tek keer on 'im long ez he lived. I
kyar'd 'im 'way off de battlefiel' out de way o' de
balls, an' I laid 'im down onder a big tree till I
could git somebody to ketch de sorrel for me. He
wuz cotched arfter awhile, an' I hed some money,
so I got some pine plank an' made a coffin dat even-

in', an' wrapt Marse Chan's body up in de fleg, an'
put 'im in de coffin ; but I didn' nail de top on
strong, 'cause I knowed ole missis wan' see 'im ;
an' I got a' ambulance an' set out for home dat
night. We reached dyar de nex' evenin', arfter
travellin' all dat night an' all nex' day.

" Hit 'peared like somethin' hed tole ole missis
we wuz comin' so ; for when we got home she wuz
waitin' for us—done drest up in her best Sunday-
clo'es, an' stan'in' at de head o' de big steps, an'
ole marster settin' in his big cheer—ez we druv
up de hill to'ds de house, I drivin' de ambulance
an' de sorrel leadin' 'long behine wid de stirrups
crost over de saddle.

" She come down to de gate to meet us. We
took de coffin out de ambulance an' kyar'd it right
into de big parlor wid de pictures in it, whar dey
use' to dance in ole times when Marse Chan wuz a
school-boy, an' Miss Anne Chahmb'lin use' to
come over, an' go wid ole missis into her chamber
an' tek her things off. In dyar we laid de coffin
on two o' de cheers, an' ole missis nuvver said a
wud ; she jes' looked so ole an' white.

" When I had tell 'em all 'bout it, I tu'ned right
'roun' an' rid over to Cun'l Chahmb'lin's, 'cause I
knowed dat wuz what Marse Chan he'd 'a' wanted
me to do. I didn' tell nobody whar I wuz gwine,
'cause yo' know none on 'em hadn' nuvver speak
to Miss Anne, not sence de duil, an' dey didn'
know 'bout de letter.

" When I rid up in de yard, dyar wuz Miss Anne

a-stan'in' on de poach watchin' me ez I rid up. I
tied my hoss to de fence, an' walked up de parf.
She knowed by de way I walked dyar wuz somethin' de motter, an' she wuz mighty pale. I drapt
my cap down on de een' o' de steps an' went up.
She nuvver opened her mouf ; jes' stan' right still
an' keep her eyes on my face. Fust, I couldn'
speak ; den I cotch my voice, an' I say, ' Marse
Chan, he done got he furlough.'

" Her face was mighty ashy, an' she sort o'
shook, but she didn' fall. She tu'ned roun' an'
said, ' Git me de ker'ige !' Dat wuz all.

" When de ker'ige come 'roun', she hed put on
her bonnet, an' wuz ready. Ez she got in, she sey
to me, ' Hev yo' brought him home ? ' an' we
drove 'long, I ridin' behine.

" When we got home, she got out, an' walked
up de big walk—up to de poach by herse'f. Ole
missis hed done fin' de letter in Marse Chan's
pocket, wid de love in it, while I wuz 'way, an' she
wuz a-waitin' on de poach. Dey sey dat wuz de
fust time ole missis cry when she find de letter, an'
dat she sut'n'y did cry over it, pintedly.

" Well, seh, Miss Anne she walks right up de
steps, mos' up to ole missis stan'in' dyar on de
poach, an' jes' falls right down mos' to her, on her
knees fust, an' den flat on her face right on de flo',
ketchin' at ole missis' dress wid her two han's—so.

" Ole missis stood for 'bout a minit lookin'
down at her, an' den she drapt down on de flo' by
her, an' took her in bofe her arms.

"I couldn' see, I wuz cryin' so myse'f, an' ev'y-body wuz cryin'. But dey went in arfter a while in de parlor, an' shet de do'; an' I hyard 'em say, Miss Anne she tuk de coffin in her arms an' kissed it, an' kissed Marse Chan, an' call 'im by his name, an' her darlin', an' ole missis lef' her cryin' in dyar tell some on 'em went in, an' found her done faint on de flo'.

"Judy (she's my wife) she tell me she heah Miss Anne when she axed ole missis mout she wear mo'nin' fur 'im. I don' know how dat is ; but when we buried 'im nex' day, she wuz de one whar walked arfter de coffin, holdin' ole marster, an' ole missis she walked next to 'em."

"Well, we buried Marse Chan dyar in de ole grabeyard, wid de fleg wrapped roun' 'im, an' he face lookin' like it did dat mawnin' down in de low groun's, wid de new sun shinin' on it so peaceful.

"Miss Anne she nuvver went home arfter dat ; she stay wid ole marster an' ole missis ez long ez dey lived. Dat warn' so mighty long, 'cause ole marster he died dat fall, when dey wuz fallerin' fur wheat—I had jes' married Judy den—an' ole missis she warn' long behine him. We buried her by him next summer. Miss Anne she went in de hospitals toreckly arfter ole missis died ; an' jes' fo' Richmond fell she come home sick wid de fever. Yo' nuvver would 'a' knowed her fur de same ole Miss Anne. She wuz light ez a piece o' peth, an' so white, 'cep' her eyes an' her sorrel

hyar, an' she kep' on gittin' whiter an' weaker.
Judy she sut'n'y did nuss her faithful. But she
nuvver got no betterment ! De fever an' Marse
Chan's bein' kilt hed done strain her, an' she died
jes' 'fo' de folks wuz sot free.

"So we buried Miss Anne right by Marse Chan,
in a place whar ole missis hed tole us to leave, an'
dey's bofe on 'em sleep side by side over in de ole
grabeyard at home.

"An' will yo' please tell me, marster ? Dey
tells me dat de Bible sey dyar won' be marryin'
nor givin' in marriage in heaven, but I don' b'lieve
it signifies dat—does yo' ?"

I gave him the comfort of my earnest belief in
some other interpretation, together with several
spare "eighteen-pences," as he called them, for
which he seemed humbly grateful. And as I rode
away I heard him calling across the fence to his
wife, who was standing in the door of a small
whitewashed cabin, near which we had been standing for some time :

"Judy, have Marse Chan's dawg got home ?"

MR. BIXBY'S CHRISTMAS VISITOR.

By Charles S. Gage.

A T the head of the first flight of stairs, and on opposite sides of the landing, were the respective rooms of Mr. Bixby and Mr. Bangs. The house in which they lived stood in a quiet and retired street on the lower and western side of New York, a locality which was once inhabited by fashionable families, afterward by old-fashioned families, and at the time of our story by the keepers of boarding-houses for single men.

Mr. Henry Bixby and Mr. Alfred Bangs were single men—Mr. Bangs, the wine-merchant, because he liked wine and song so well that he never had leisure to think of women, because he was fat, because he was red in the face, and, if more reasons are necessary, because his fingers were chubby and short. For twenty years, day by day, Mr. Bangs had been absorbed in business.

•*• *Appleton's Journal, December* 30, 1871.

For twenty years, night after night, it had been his custom to entertain his friends at his apartment in not a very quiet way. He was so happy, and bulbous, and jolly, that he had never thought of marriage. Yet he might easily have been mistaken by the casual observer for a family man. He wore a white vest when it wasn't too cold ; his linen was painfully plain. There was not a sign of jewelry about him. He wore low shoes, which he tied with a ribbon. This was Mr. Bangs.

Not quite so old in years as the opposite lodger was Mr. Bixby, known to his few friends as a genial philosopher and poet, to the public as the literary critic of one of the great daily papers. He might have been thirty-five years of age, but, as he had lived more for others than for himself, as he had made a study and not a pleasure of life, his gray eyes and the other features of his face suggested to whoever met him a longer past. There was something about him that caused men to wonder, not what he was, but what he had been.

For ten years Mr. Bangs and Mr. Bixby had been inmates of the house together. Mr. Bangs had been there longer. The present landlady had received as a legacy from her predecessor, who did not care to take him away, Mr. Bangs. As she ·said, she made a present of Bangs.

Long as they had known each other, the two lodgers were only acquaintances. Sometimes, on a Sunday afternoon, they would walk out in company, stroll down to the Battery, and there smoke their cigars and watch the ships, but beyond this point of sociability, which neither enjoyed, there was nothing more. Never had Bixby read Bangs any poem he had made, nor did ever Bangs invite Bixby to meet his convivial friends of an evening to play whist or to partake of his mulled ale. In fact, Mr. Bixby had been often and with great enthusiasm voted an unsocial fellow by the cronies of Mr. Bangs, but he rose somewhat in their estimation when they were informed that he had consented to exchange rooms with their host.

"He isn't such a grouty fellow, after all," said Bangs. "I told him that we were too near the street, and that some one had been complaining to the landlady of our singing. He didn't even stop to think, but agreed to do it at once. He thought the light would be better here. Now, fellows, I call that doing the fair thing."

And the speech of Mr. Bangs was applauded.

It was the morning of the day before Christmas that the change was effected. In the closet where had been the bottles, the decanters, glasses, and pickle-jars of the late occupant, Mr. Bixby had arranged shelves, and filled them with his books. Over the mantel, from which Mr. Bangs had taken away a colored print of a bull-dog in an overcoat, Mr. Bixby hung a fine engraving of the Madonna, . and on the mantel itself he had placed his clock. It was a small French clock under a crystal, so that its rapidly-swinging pendulum could be easily seen. All bachelors, however negligent of their surroundings, have some one hobby among articles of furniture. It may be an easy-chair, or a book-case, or a chandelier—there is one thing that must be the best of its kind. There could be no doubt, from the care with which Mr. Bixby placed his clock in its position, and from time to time compared it with his watch, that this was his hobby. It had the three requisites which he demanded in a clock. It kept correct time without failing, its pendulum swung rapidly, and was plainly visible. Time past was the happiness of Mr. Bixby, and this clock told him continually that all was being done that could be done to induce the hours of every day to go over to the majority. He depended upon this clock. He was surer of its mechanism than of that of his own heart.

What with hanging his pictures and arranging his furniture, and with many other little things which had to be done, Mr. Bixby was busily employed all day. But the task was not an unpleasant one. His heart was in the work, for there was hardly an object in the room not nearly associated with some event in his past life. After carefully brushing the dust from an old writing-desk, which had evidently once belonged to a lady, he placed it upon the rug in front of the fire. Only on Christmas-eves was this desk opened.

"It is curious," thought Mr. Bixby, "that I should have moved this day, of all days in the year!"

Often in his work he thought of stopping to take

from the desk an old packet of letters, and reading them once more. But it was not yet time, and, moreover, he was continually interrupted. First, there came some one to his door with " Two dozen Congress-water for Mr. Bangs ;" then one with " Mr. Bangs's boots," and another to tell Mr. Bangs that " the pup was big enough to take away." Finally, came Bangs himself, to complain of like interruptions, and to bid him good-by.

" Here is some manuscript a boy left for you. You will have to attend both doors now. I am off to spend Christmas. We are going to have a Tom-and-Jerry party in Jersey. You know—

> " 'The Tom-and-Jerry days have come, the happiest in the year !'

Good rendering, eh ? That isn't all :

> " ' I only wish to live till the juleps come again ! ' "

And Mr. Bangs laughed uproariously, even after he had said, " Good-by," and shut the door behind him.

" What a personification of Bacchus !" thought Mr. Bixby—

> " ' Ever laughing, ever young.'

He will be young as long as he lives, but I am afraid that won't be long. If ever there was a man in immediate danger of apoplexy, Bangs is that man."

It was after dinner when Mr. Bixby lighted his drop-light and sat down before the fire. He pushed an ottoman in front of him, on which to rest his feet, which he had comfortably encased in his slippers. But the shadows in his new room did not please him. He could hardly see the clock on the mantel. The Madonna above was completely in the shade. So he lighted the chandelier above and sat down again, hoping that no friend, either of his own or of Mr. Bangs, would interrupt him. The desk was open at his feet. The package of letters lay near him on the table. He placed his hand upon them, but let it rest there. The hour had not quite arrived when he would read them. He fell again into the reveries of the day. He lingered over the thoughts of his better life ere he opened the packet which told of its end. For the last ten years he had labored without ambition, and had been successful. His name was well known as a journalist, and his salary was ample. Before that time he had striven ambitiously, but fruitlessly, patiently, but as in a quicksand, until, on a day, he had none to strive for but himself, and then success had come. Since noon, seven hours and twenty-nine minutes, said the clock before him. His anniversary was near. Mr. Bixby drew the letters near him, and untied the package. Just then there came a knock at his door, and, before he had determined whether or not he should say, "Come in," the door opened, and an elderly gentleman stepped into the apartment. Quietly he came in. There was no sound attending his entrance except the knock. Mr.

Bixby, looking up, saw a man of more than ordinary height, with countenance rigid and puritanical in expression, as though the mind which had formed it was one influenced more by justice than mercy. His eyes were concealed by a pair of colored spectacles, but these, as they caught and reflected the light, were brighter and more startling than any eyes could have been. He was dressed in a long surtout, which he wore closely buttoned, high dickey, and high black-silk stock, which covered his throat to his chin. His iron-gray hair was brushed somewhat pompously backward over his forehead, and his whole effect was that of a gentleman of the generation which wore bell-crowned hats and carried enormous canes with tassels. But what attracted Mr. Bixby's particular attention were the wrinkles of his face. These were in all places where wrinkles should not be. One ran straight through the centre of his forehead, continuing the line of the nose upward to the hair. Two others, starting from the bridge of the nose, ran diagonally down to the nostrils. He was close-shaven, and his lips were straight and thin. These peculiarities of his visitor Mr. Bixby had barely time to mark when the gentleman said :

"Ah, Mr. Bangs, I am glad to find you in !"

Mr. Bixby never in his life more desired to be alone, and yet there was something in this old man which so attracted him that he could not correct his mistake. He felt a sudden fascination and desire to know more of him. Bangs was away and could not be seen. The gentleman could not be very well acquainted with Bangs, very probably never had seen him, or he would not have made such an error. But nothing but the influence which seemed to proceed from his visitor could have induced Mr. Bixby to answer as he did.

" Thank you, sir. Pray, take this chair."

As he said this, he arose and wheeled an easy-chair to the other side of the table.

The elderly gentleman sat down.

" You have a very cheerful apartment here, Mr. Bangs."

" Yes. I always like to be comfortable."

" Of course," said the elderly gentleman.

" Will you remove your overcoat, sir ?" asked Mr. Bixby, and immediately repented it.

" Oh, no, I shall stop but a moment."

There was an interval of silence. A block of coal broke open in the grate and fell apart. A jet of gas burst forth and burned, then sputtered and went out. Mr. Bixby wondered on what business he had come, and why he did not open the subject at once, if he was only intending to stop a moment.

" It is very disagreeable weather out," said the man with the pompous forelock, interrupting his reflections.

" Snowing ?" asked Bixby.

" No—sleet."

" Very unpleasant to have far to go such a

night," suggested Bixby, who could think of nothing better to say.

" Not at all," responded the old gentleman, authoritatively.

Bixby was silent again.

The old gentleman, leaning with his elbow on the table, began again.

" You like to live well, Mr. Bangs ?"

" I try to," answered Mr. Bixby.

" Yes."

" This must be some relative of Bangs come to deliver him a lecture on his course of life. Why don't he broach his advice at once ?" thought Mr. Bixby. The visitor here pulled a glove from his right hand, ran his fingers through his hair, and then, in a more business-like tone, spoke again :

" Although a stranger to you personally, Mr. Bangs, I have always taken a great interest in your family. Mr. Bangs, I knew your father."

" Indeed ! I never heard him speak—"

" No, I dare say ; it was near the end of his life. I was near by, and rendered him some assistance, when he died suddenly of apoplexy. He was not so much of a man as your grandfather."

" Was he not ?" asked Mr. Bixby, musingly. He was thinking how old the grandfather of his friend Bangs must have been.

" No," continued the elderly gentleman ; " but even his judgment I never considered equal to that of your great-grandfather."

" Here is, indeed, a friend—a friend of the

family. Why is Mr. Bangs away ?" thought Mr.
Bixby, and he bent his head a little, and looked
under the drop-light, to get a view of his visitor.
He saw only the reflection on his spectacles, and
drew back suddenly, for fear of being detected.

"You like a good song, I have heard, Mr.
Bangs," came from the other side of the table.
"Have you any favorite ?"

Mr. Bixby did not understand this at all. The
question puzzled him. Should he as Bangs fall in
the estimation of some relative if he admitted the
fact ? Or did his visitor intend to sing ? However, he felt compelled to be frank, so he said :

"Oh, yes ; I like a good song. Some of the
Scotch ballads please me most. There is ' The
Land o' the Leal.' "

"A very fine song, sir. A very fine song. It is
a credit to any man to like that song."

The old gentleman was excited. Mr. Bixby was
just congratulating himself on having given Bangs
a lift, when his thoughts were turned into an altogether new channel by the following remark :

"It was my impression, however, that your taste
ran rather in the way of drinking-songs. I should
have thought now you would have said, ' The
Coal-Black Wine.' "

There was something in the tone with which this
was uttered that made Mr. Bixby shudder. It ran
through his mind that this man was some enemy
of Bangs—that he was dangerous. Startled by
this sudden suspicion, tremblingly he again peered

under the shade. The wrinkle in the line of the frontal suture was more deeply indented. The light on the spectacles was brighter than ever.

"Mr. Bangs, I called on your opposite neighbor, Mr. Bixby, to-night. I knocked on the door, but he was away."

"Yes," said Mr. Bixby, somewhat confused. He wished that Bangs had stayed at home, and determined to end the interview as soon as possible.

"Yes. I am sorry. I had a positive appointment with him. I am a great friend of his."

"Does he know you?"

"Oh, no; we have never met personally that he remembers. I am an old friend of the family. He suffers from the heart-disease, and has been expecting me."

"Oh, you are a physician?"

"Yes, sir. I attended his father at his last illness."

Mr. Bixby's heart began to beat rapidly. His mind became equally active, and, although he had no experience to be guided by, he began to suspect the nature of this man's business with Bangs. He almost determined to discover himself, but the letters were yet unread. If that were only done, he would do anything his visitor might request. Recalling the old gentleman's last words, he said, at last, calmly:

"And his mother?"

"Yes, and his mother."

The old man's voice assumed almost a kindly tone.

"He is, indeed, a friend of my family," thought Mr. Bixby ; and then he started, for fear he might have spoken aloud.

His eyes fell upon the packet of letters. He must read them. He must end the interview. The old doctor must have noticed Mr. Bixby's eyes, with the tears rising in them, as he tenderly touched the letters one by one, for it was with a voice very gentle and low that he spoke again.

"I attended once a very dear friend of his. It must be quite ten years ago now. Her name was Margaret. I think she loved him, for I remember —yes—it was one Christmas-eve, she said, and after that she said no more, ' Has Harry come ? ' "

Mr. Bixby could bear no more. His sobs were striving for utterance. His fingers grasped the strong oak arms of his chair. It was only the thought of the letters which gave him strength to say :

"I am sorry, sir. You mistake me. I must ask you to leave me. You may come again. I shall be here, but I have something I would do to-night. I have given you much of my time. It is already late."

"It is you who mistake, Mr. Bangs. But I am going now. I said I would stop but a moment. I have kept my promise, as you will see by your clock."

Before his hands fell listless from the arms of

the chair—before his lips parted, but not for speech
—ay, just before that quick, strong pain in his
heart, Mr. Bixby saw on the white dial the black
hands yet pointing to the seven hours and the
twenty-nine minutes, the pendulum moveless, still,
half-way on the upward journey of the arc.

The elderly gentleman arose, walked round the
table, and smiled, himself, as he saw a smile of
perfected happiness on the face of the dead, when
so lately sorrow itself had been pictured on the
face of the living.

"It was hard to deceive him, but he will thank
me now," said he of the gray locks and wrinkled
visage. "And here are the letters which he does
not need."

Had the old man no more appointments to keep?
For he took up one of the letters and opened it.
A lock of golden hair fell unnoticed to the floor.
Then he read silently, and, after a while, aloud :

"I hope you will come and see me on Christmas-
eve, for I am not well. I long for you more than
I can say. You must be tired with your struggle
in the great city, and need rest. O Harry ! come
and comfort her that loves you, as you well know.

"MARGARET."

The bells of Trinity commenced ringing.

"He was tired, and he needed rest," said Death.

ELI.

BY C. H. WHITE.

I.

UNDER a boat, high and dry, at low tide, on the beach, John Wood was seated in the sand, sheltered from the sun in the boat's shadow, absorbed in the laying on of verdigris. The dull, worn color was rapidly giving place to a brilliant, shining green. Occasionally a scraper, which lay by, was taken up to remove the last trace of a barnacle.

It was Wood's boat, but he was not a boatman ; he painted cleverly, but he was not a painter. He kept the brown store under the elms of the main street, now hot and still, where at this moment his blushing sister was captivating the heart of an awkward farmer's boy, as she sold him a pair of striped suspenders.

.*. *Century Magazine, November,* 1881.

As the church-clock struck the last of twelve decided blows, three children came rushing out of the house on the bank above the beach. It was one of those deceptive New England cottages, weather-worn without, but bright and bountifully home-like within—with its trim parlor, proud of a cabinet organ ; with its front hall, now cooled by the light sea-breeze drifting through the blind-door, where a tall clock issued its monotonous call to a siesta on the rattan lounge ; with its spare room, open now, opposite the parlor, and now, too, drawing in the salt air through close-shut blinds, in anticipation of the joyful arrival this evening of Sister Sarah, with her little brood, from the city.

The children scampered across the road, and then the eldest hushed the others and sent a little brother ahead to steal, barefoot, along the shining sea-weed to his father.

The plotted surprise appeared to succeed completely. The painter was seized by the ears from behind, and captured.

" Guess who's here, or you can't get up," said the infant captor.

" It's Napoleon Bonaparte ; don't joggle," said his father, running a brush steadily along the water-line.

" No ! no ! no !" with shouts of laughter from the whole attacking party.

" Then it's Captain Ezekiel ?"

This excited great merriment : Captain Ezekiel

was an aged, purblind man, who leaned on a
cane.

After attempts to identify the invader — with
the tax-collector come for taxes, then with the
elderly minister making a pastoral call, with the
formal schoolmaster, and with Samuel J. Tilden
—the victim reached over his shoulder, and, seizing
the assailant by a handful of calico jacket, brought
him around, squirming, before him.

" Now," he said, " I'll give you a coat of verdigris."

(Great applause from the reserve force behind.)

" I suppose Mother sent you to say dinner's
ready," said the father, rising and surveying the
green bottom of the boat. " I must eat quick, so
as to do the other side before half-flood."

And with a child on each shoulder, and the third
pushing him from behind with her head, he
marched toward the vine-covered kitchen, where,
between two opposite netted doors, the table was
trimly set.

" Father, you look like a mermaid, with your
green hands," said his wife, laughing, as she
handed him the spirits of turpentine. " A woman
could paint that boat, in a light dress, and not get
a spot on her."

He smiled good-naturedly : he never spoke
much.

" I guess Louise won't have much trade to-day,"
said his wife, as they all sat down ; " it's so hot
in the sun that everybody'll wait till night. But

she has her tatting-work to do, and she's got a book, too, that she wanted to finish."

Her husband nodded, and ate away.

"Oh, can't we go up street and see her, this afternoon?" said one of the children.

"Who can that be?" said the mother, as an elderly, half-official-looking man stopped his horse at the front gate and alighted. The man left the horse unchecked to browse by the road-side, and came to the door.

"Oh, it's you, Captain Nourse," said Wood, rising to open the netting door, and holding out his hand. "Come to summons me as a witness in something about the bank case, I suppose. Let me introduce Captain Nourse, Mary," he said, "deputy sheriff. Sit down, Captain, and have some dinner with us."

"No, I guess I won't set," said the captain. "I cal'lated not to eat till I got home, in the middle o' the a'ternoon. No, I'll set down in eye-shot of the mare, and read the paper while you eat."

"I hope they don't want me to testify anywhere to-day," said Wood; "because my boat's half verdigris'd, and I want to finish her this afternoon."

"No testimony to-day," said the captain. "Hi! hi! Kitty!" he called to the mare, as she began to meander across the road; and he went out to a tree by the front fence, and sat down on a green bench, beside a work-basket and a half-finished child's dress, and read the country paper which he had taken from the office as he came along.

After dinner Wood went out bareheaded, and leaned on the fence by the captain. His wife stood just inside the door, looking out at them.

The " bank case " was the great sensation of the town, and Wood was one of the main witnesses, for he had been taking the place of the absent cashier when the safe was broken open and rifled, to the widespread distress of depositors and stock-holders and the ruin of Hon. Edward Clark, the president. Wood had locked the safe on the after-noon before the eventful night, and had carried home the key with him, and he was to testify to the contents of the safe as he had left it.

" I guess they're glad they've got such a witness as John," said his wife to herself, as she looked at him fondly, "and I guess they think there won't be much doubt about what he says."

" Well, Captain," said Wood, jocosely, breaking a spear of grass to bits in his fingers, " I didn't know but you'd come to arrest me."

The captain calmly smiled as only a man can smile who has been accosted with the same humor-ous remark a dozen times a day for twenty years. He folded his paper carefully, put it in his pocket, took off his spectacles and put them in their silver case, took a red silk handkerchief from his hat, wiped his face, and put the handkerchief back. Then he said, shortly :

" That's what I *have* come for."

Wood, still leaning on the fence, looked at him, and said nothing.

" That's just what I've come for," said Captain

Nourse. " I've got to arrest you ; here's the warrant." And he handed it to him.

" What does this mean ?" said Wood. " I can't make head nor tail of this."

" Well," said the captain, " the long and short is : these high-toned detectives that they've had down from town, seein' as our own force wasn't good enough, allow that the safe was unlocked with a key, in due form, and then the lock was broke afterward, to look as if it had been forced open. They've had the foreman of the safe-men down, too, and he says the same thing. Naturally, the argument is : there were only two keys in existence ; one was safe with the president of the bank, and is about all he's got to show out of forty years' savings ; the only other one you had : consequently it heaves it on to you."

" I see," said Wood. " I will go with you. Do you want to come into the house with me while I get my coat ?"

" Well, I suppose I must keep you in sight— now, you know."

And they went into the house.

" Mary," said her husband, " the folks that lost by Clark when the bank broke have been at him until he's felt obliged to pitch on somebody, and he's pitched on me ; and Captain Nourse has come to arrest me. I shall get bail before long."

She said nothing, and did not shed a tear till he was gone.

But then——

II.

WIDE wastes of salt marsh to the right, imprison-
ing the upland with a vain promise of infinite
liberty, and, between low, distant sand-hills, a rim
of sea.   Stretches of pine woods behind, shutting
in from the great outer world, and soon to darken
into evening gloom. Ploughed fields and elm-dotted
pastures to the left, and birch-lined roads leading
by white farm-houses to the village, all speaking
of cheer and freedom to the prosperous and the
happy, but to the unfortunate and the indebted, of
meshes invisible but strong as steel.   But, before,
no lonesome marshes, no desolate forest, no farm
or village street, but the free blue ocean, rolling
and tumbling still from the force of an expended
gale.

In the open door-way of a little cottage, warmed
by the soft slanting rays of the September sun, a
rough man, burnt and freckled, was sitting, at his
feet a net, engaged upon some handiwork which
two little girls were watching.   Close by him lay
a setter, his nose between his paws.   Occasionally
the man raised his eyes to scan the sea.

" There's Joel," he said, " comin' in around the
Bar.   Not much air stirrin' now !"

Then he turned to his work again.

" First, you go *so* fash'," he said to the children,
as he drew a thread ; " then you go *so* fash'."

And as he worked he made a great show of labor, much to their diversion.

But the sight of Joel's broad white sail had not brought pleasant thoughts to his mind. For Joel had hailed him, off the Shoal, the afternoon before, and had obligingly offered to buy his fish, right there, and so let him go directly home, omitting to mention that sudden jump of price due to an empty market.

"Wonder what poor man he's took a dollar out of to-day! Well, I s'pose it's all right: those that's got money, want money."

"What be you; Eli—ganging on hooks?" said Aunt Patience, as she tip-toed into the kitchen behind him, from his wife's sick-room, and softly closed the door after her.

"No," said the elder of the children; "he's mending our stockings, and showing me how."

"Well, you do have a hard time, don't you?" said Aunt Patience, looking down over his shoulder; "to slave and tug and scrape to get a house over your head, and then to have to turn square 'round, and stay to home with a sick woman, and eat all into it with mortgages!"

"Oh, well," he said, "we'll fetch, somehow."

Aunt Patience went to the glass, and holding a black pin in her mouth, carefully tied the strings of her sun-bonnet.

"Anyway," she says, "you take it good-natured. Though if there is one thing that's harder than another, it is to be good-natured all

the time, without being aggravating. I have
known men that was so awfully good-natured that
they was harder to live with than if they was
cross !''

And without specifying further, she opened her
plaid parasol, and stepped out at the porch.

THOUGH, on this quiet afternoon of Saturday,
the peace of the approaching Sabbath seemed
already brooding over the little dwelling, peace
had not lent her hand to the building of the home.
Every foot of land, every shingle, every nail, had
been wrung from the reluctant sea. Every voyage
had contributed something. It was a great day
when Eli was able to buy the land. Then, between
two voyages, he dug a cellar and laid a founda-
tion ; then he saved enough to build the main part
of the cottage and to finish the front room, lending
his own hand to the work. Then he used to get
letters at every port, telling of progress—how
Lizzie, his wife, had adorned the front room with
a bright nine-penny paper, of which a little piece
was inclosed, which he kept as a sort of charm
about him and exhibited to his friends ; how she
and her little brother had lathed the entry and the
kitchen, and how they had set out blackberry vines
from the woods. Then another letter told of a
surprise awaiting him on his return ; and, in due
time, coming home as third mate from Hong Kong
to a seaman's tumultuous welcome, he had found
that a great, good-natured mason, with whose sick

child his wife had watched, night after night, had appeared one day with lime and hair and sand, and in white raiment, and had plastered the entry and the kitchen, and finished a room upstairs.

And so, for years, at home and on the sea, at New York, and at Valparaiso, and in the Straits of Malacca, the little house and the little family within it had grown into the fibre of Eli's heart. Nothing had given him more delight than to meet, in the strange streets of Calcutta or before the Mosque of Omar, some practical Yankee from Stonington or Machias, and, whittling, to discuss with him, among the turbans of the Orient, the comparative value of shaved and of sawed shingles, or the economy of " Swedes-iron" nails, and to go over with him the estimates and plans which he had worked out in his head under all the constellations of the skies.

THE supper things were cleared away. The children had said good-night and gone to bed, and Eli had been sitting for an hour by his wife's bedside. He had had to tax his patience and ingenuity heavily during the long months that she had lain there to entertain her for a little while in the evening, after his hard, wet day's work. He had been talking now of the coming week, when he was to serve upon the jury in the adjoining county-town.

" I cal'late I can come home about every night," he said, " and it'll be quite a change, at any rate."

" But you don't seem so cheerful about it as I

counted you would be," said his wife. " Are you afraid you'll have to be on the bank-case ?"

" Not much !" he answered. " No trouble 'n that case ! Jury won't leave their seats. These city fellers'll find they've bit off more'n they can chew when they try to figure out John Wood done that. I only hope I'll have the luck to be on that case—all hands on the jury whisper together a minute, and then clear him, right on the spot, and then shake hands with him all 'round ! "

" But something is worrying you," she said. " What is it ? You have looked it since noon."

" Oh, nothin'," he replied — " only George Cahoon came up to-noon to say that he was goin' West next week, and that he would have to have that money he let me have a while ago. And where to get it—I don't know,"

III.

THE court-room was packed. John Wood's trial was drawing to its close. Eli was on the jury. Some one had advised the prosecuting attorney, in a whisper, to challenge him, but he had shaken his head and said :

" Oh, I couldn't afford to challenge him for that ; it would only leak out, and set the jury against me. I'll risk his standing out against this evidence."

The trial had been short. It had been shown how

the little building of the bank had been entered. Skilled locksmiths from the city had testified that the safe was opened with a key, and that the lock was broken afterward, from the inside—plainly to raise the theory of a forcible entry by strangers.

It had been proved that the only key in existence, not counting that kept by the president, was in the possession of Wood, who was filling, for a few days, the place of the cashier—the president's brother—in his absence. It had been shown that Wood was met, at one o'clock of the night in question, crossing the fields toward his home, from the direction of the bank, with a large wicker basket slung over his shoulders, returning, as he had said, from eel-spearing in Harlow's Creek ; and there was other circumstantial evidence.

Mr. Clark, the president of the bank, had won the sympathy of every one by the modest way in which, with eye-glasses in hand, he had testified to the particulars of the loss which had left him penniless, and had ruined others whose little all was in his hands. And then, in reply to the formal question, he had testified, amid roars of laughter from the court-room, that it was not he who robbed the safe. At this, even the judge and Wood's lawyer had not restrained a smile.

This had left the guilt with Wood. His lawyer, an inexperienced young attorney—who had done more or less business for the bank, and would hardly have ventured to defend this case but that the president had kindly expressed his entire will-

ingness that he should do so—had, of course, not
thought it worth while to cross-examine Mr. Clark,
and had directed his whole argument against the
theory that the safe had been opened with a key,
and not by strangers. But he had felt all through
that, as a man politely remarked to him when he
finished, he was only butting his " head ag'in a
stone wall."

And while he was arguing, a jolly-looking old
lawyer had written, in the fly-leaf of a law-book on
his knee, and passed with a wink to a young man
near him who had that very morning been
admitted to the bar, these lines :

> " When callow Blackstones soar too high,
>   Quit common-sense, and reckless fly,
>   Soon, Icarus-like, they headlong fall,
>   And down come client, case, and all."

The district-attorney had not thought it worth
while to expend much strength upon his closing
argument ; but being a jovial stump-speaker, of a
wide reputation within narrow limits, he had not
been able to refrain from making merry over
Wood's statement that the basket which he had
been seen bearing home, on the eventful night, was
a basket of eels.

" Fine eels those, gentlemen ! We have seen
gold-fish and silver-fish, but golden eels are first
discovered by this defendant. The apostle, in
Holy Writ, caught a fish with a coin in its mouth ;
but this man leaves the apostle in the dim distance

when he finds eels that are all money. No storied
fisherman of Bagdad, catching enchanted princes
disguised as fishes in the sea, ever hooked such a
treasure as this defendant hooked when he hooked
that basket of eels ! [Rustling appreciation of the
pun among the jury.] If a squirming, twisting,
winding, wriggling eel, gentleman, can be said at
any given moment to have a back, we may distin-
guish this new-found species as the green-back eel.
It is a common saying that no man can hold an eel
and remain a Christian. I should like to have
viewed the pious equanimity of this church-mem-
ber when he laid his hands on that whole bed of
eels. In happy, barefoot boyhood, gentlemen, we
used to find mud-turtles marked with initials or de-
vices cut in their shells ; but what must have been
our friend's surprise to find, in the muddy bed of
Harlow's Creek, eels marked with a steel-engraving
of the landing of Columbus, and the signature of
the Register of the Treasury ! I hear that a cor-
poration is now being formed by the title of The
Harlow's Creek Greenback National Bank-bill Eel-
fishing Company, to follow up, with seines and
spears, our worthy friend's discovery ! I learn that
the news of this rich placer has spread to the
golden mountains of the West, and that the ex-
hausted intellects which have been reduced to such
names for their mines as ' The Tombstone,' ' The
Red Dog,' the ' Mrs. E. J. Parkhurst,' are likely
now to flood us with prospectuses of the ' Eel
Mine,' ' The Flat Eel,' ' The Double Eel,' and then,

when they get ready to burst upon confiding friends, ' The Consolidated Eels.' "

It takes but little to make a school or a court-room laugh, and the speech had appeared to give a good deal of amusement to the listeners.

To all ?

Did it amuse that man who sat, with folded arms, harsh and rigid, at the dock ? Did it divert that white-faced woman, cowering in a corner, listening as in a dream ?

THE judge now charged the jury briefly. It was unnecessary for him, he said, to recapitulate evidence of so simple a character. The chief question for the jury was as to the credibility of the witnesses. If the witnesses for the prosecution were truthful and were not mistaken, the inference of guilt seemed inevitable ; this the defendant's counsel had conceded. The defendant had proved a good reputation ; upon that point there was only this to be said : that, while such evidence was entitled to weight, yet, on the other hand, crimes involving a breach of trust could, from their very nature, be committed only by persons whose good reputations secured them positions of trust.

THE jury-room had evidently not been furnished by a ring. There was a long table for debate, twelve hard chairs for repose, twelve spittoons for luxury, and a clock.

The jury sat in silence for a few moments, as

old Captain Nourse, who had them in his keeping,
and eyed them as if he was afraid that he might lose
one of them in a crack and be held accountable on
his bond, rattled away at the unruly lock. Looking at them then, you would have seen faces all of
a New England cast but one. There was a tall,
powerful negro called George Washington, a man
well known in this county town, to which he had
come, as driftwood from the storm of war, in '65.
Some of the "boys" had heard him, in a great
prayer-meeting in Washington—a city which he
always spoke of as his "namesake"—at the time
of the great review, say, in his strong voice, with
that pathetic quaver in it : "Like as de parched
an' weary traveller hangs his harp upon de winder,
an' sighs for oysters in de desert, so I longs to
res' my soul an' my foot in Mass'chusetts ;" and
they were so delighted with him that they invited
him on the spot to go home with them, and took
up a collection to pay his fare, and so he was a
public character. As for his occupation—when the
census-taker, with a wink to the boys in the store,
had asked him what it was, he had said, in that
same odd tone : "Putties up glass a little—white-
washes a little—" and, when the man had made a
show of writing all that down, "preaches a little."
He might have said "preaches a big," for you
could hear him half a mile away.

The foreman was a retired sea-captain. "Good
cap'n—Cap'n Thomas," one of his neighbors had
said of him. "Allers gits good ships—never hez

to go huntin' 'round for a vessel. But it is astonishin' what differences they is ! Now there's Cap'n A. K. P. Bassett, down to the West Harbor. You let it git 'round that Cap'n A. K. P. is goin' off on a Chiny voyage, and you'll see half a dozen old shays to onct, hitched all along his fence of an arternoon, and wimmen inside the house, to git Cap'n A. K. P. to take their boys. But you let Cap'n Thomas give out that he wants boys, and he hez to glean 'em—from the poor-house, and from step-mothers, and where he can : the wimmen knows ! Still," he added, "Cap'n Thomas 's a good cap'n. I've nothin' to say ag'in him. He's smart !"

"GENTLEMEN," said the foreman, when the officer, at last, had securely locked them in, "shall we go through the formality of a ballot ? If the case were a less serious one, we might have rendered a verdict in our seats."

"What's the use foolin' 'round ballotin' ?" said a thick-set butcher. "Ain't we all o' one mind ?"

"It is for you to say, gentlemen," said the foreman. "I shouldn't want to have it go abroad that we had not acted formally, if there was any one disposed to cavil."

"Mr. Speaker," said George Washington, rising and standing in the attitude of Webster, "I rises to appoint to order. We took ballast in de prior cases, and why make flesh of one man an' a fowl of another ?"

"Very well," said the foreman, a trifle sharply.
"'The longest way round is the shortest way
home.'"

Twelve slips of paper were handed out, to be indorsed guilty, "for form." They were collected
in a hat and the foreman told them over—"just
for form." "'Guilty,' 'guilty,' 'guilty,' 'guilty';
—wait a minute," he said, "here is a mistake.
Here is one 'not guilty'—whose is this?"

There was a pause.

"Whose is it?" said the foreman, sharply.

Eli turned a little red.

"It's mine," he said.

"Do you mean it?" said the foreman.

"Of course I mean it," he answered.

"Whew!" whistled the foreman. "Very well,
sir; we'll have an understanding, then. This case
is proved to the satisfaction of every man who
heard it, I may safely say, but one. Will that one
please state the grounds of his opinion?'

"I ain't no talker," said Eli, "but I ain't satisfied he's guilty—that's all."

"Don't you believe the witnesses?"

"Mostly."

"Which one don't you believe?"

"I can't say. I don't believe he's guilty."

"Is there one that you think lied?"

No answer.

"Now it seems to me——" said a third juryman.

"One thing at a time, gentlemen," said the
foreman. "Let us wait for an answer from Mr.

Smith. Is there any one that you think lied ? We will wait, gentlemen, for an answer."

There was a long pause. The trial seemed to Eli Smith to have shifted from the court to this shabby room, and he was now the culprit.

All waited for him ; all eyes were fixed upon him.

The clock ticked loud ! Eli counted the seconds. He knew the determination of the foreman.

The silence became intense.

" I want to say my say," said a short man in a pea-jacket—a retired San Francisco pilot, named Eldridge. " I entertain no doubt the man is guilty. At the same time, I allow for differences of opinion. I don't know this man that's voted ' not guilty,' but he seems to be a well-meaning man. I don't know his reasons ; probably he don't understand the case. I should like to have the foreman tell the evidence over, so as if he don't see it clear, he can ask questions, and we can explain."

" I second de motion," said George Washington.

There was a general rustle of approval.

" I move it," said the pilot, encouraged.

" Very well, Mr. Eldridge," said the foreman. " If there is no objection, I will state the evidence, and if there is any loop-hole, I will trouble Mr. Smith to suggest it as I go along," and he proceeded to give a summary of the testimony, with homely force.

" Now, sir ?" he said, when he had finished.

" I move for another ballot," said Mr. Eldridge.

The result was the same. Eli had voted "not guilty."

"Mr. Smith," said the foreman, "this must be settled in some way. This is no child's play. You can't keep eleven men here, trifling with them, giving no pretence of a reason."

"I haven't any reasons, only that I don't believe he's guilty," said Eli. "I'm not goin' to vote a man into states-prison, when I don't believe he done it," and he rose and walked to the window, and looked out. It was low tide. There was a broad stretch of mud in the distance, covered with boats lying over disconsolate. A driving storm had emptied the streets. He beat upon the rain-dashed glass a moment with his fingers, and then he sat down again.

"Well, sir," said the foreman, "this is singular conduct. What do you propose to do?"

Silence.

"I suppose you realize that the rest of us are pretty rapidly forming a conclusion on this matter," said the foreman.

"Come! come!" said Mr. Eldridge; "don't be quite so hard on him, Captain. Now, Mr. Smith," he said, standing up with his hands in his coat-pockets, and looking at Eli, "we know that there often is crooked sticks on juries, that hold out alone—that's to be expected; but they always argue, and stand to it the rest are fools, and all that. Now, all is, we don't see why you don't sort of argue, if you've got reasons satisfactory to

you. Come, now," he added, walking up to Eli,
and resting one foot on the seat of his chair, "why
don't you tell it over? and if we're wrong, I'm
ready to join you."

Eli looked up at him.

"Didn't you ever know," he said, "of a man's
takin' a cat off, to lose, that his little girl didn't want
drownded, and leavin' him ashore, twenty or thirty
miles, bee-line, from home, and that cat's bein'
back again the next day, purrin' 'round 's if nothin'
had happened?"

"Yes," said Mr. Eldridge—"knew of just such
a case."

"Very well," said Eli; "how does he find his
way home?"

"Don't know," said Mr. Eldridge; "always
has been a standing mystery to me."

"Well," said Eli, "mark my words. There's
such a thing as arguin', and there's such a thing as
knowin' outright; and when you'll tell me how
that cat inquires his way home, I'll tell you how I
know John Wood ain't guilty."

This made a certain sensation, and Eli's stock
went up.

An old, withered man rapped on the table.

"That's so!" he said; "and there's other
sing'lar things! How is it that a sea-farin' man,
that's dyin' to home, will allers die on the ebb-
tide? It never fails, but how does it happen? Tell
me that! And there's more ways than one of
knowin' things, too!"

"I know that man ain't guilty," said Eli.

"Hark ye!" said a dark old man with a troubled face, rising and pointing his finger toward Eli. "*Know*, you say? I *knew*, wunst. I *knew* that my girl, my only child; was good. One night she went off with a married man that worked in my store, and stole my money—and where is she now?" And then he added, "What I *know* is, that every man hes his price. I hev mine, and you hev yourn!"

The impugnment of Eli's motives was evident to all.

"'Xcuse me, Mr. Speaker," said George Washington, rising with his hand in his bosom; "as de question is befo' us, I wish to say that de las' bro' mus' have spoken under 'xcitement. Every man *don'* have his price! An' I hope de bro' will recant—like as de Psalmist goes out o' his way to say '*In my haste* I said, All men are liars.' He was a very busy man, de Psalmist—writin' down hymns all day, sharpen'n' his lead-pencil, bossin' 'roun' de choir—callin' Selah! Well, bro'n an' sisters"—both arms going out, and his voice going up—"one day, seems like, he was in gre't haste—got to finish a psalm for a monthly concert, or such—and some man incorrupted him, and lied; and bein' in gre't haste—and a little old Adam in him—he says, right off, quick : '*All* men are liars!' But see—when he gets a little time to set back and meditate, he says: 'Dis won' do—dere's Moses, an' Job, an' Paul—dey ain't liars!' An'

den he don' sneak out, and 'low he said, ' All men
is lions,' or such. No ! de Psalmist ain't no such
man ; but he owns up, an' 'xplains : ' *In my haste,*'
he says, ' I said it.' "

The foreman rose and rapped.

" I await a motion," said he, " if our friend will
allow me the privilege of speaking."

Mr. Washington calmly bowed.

Then the foreman, when nobody seemed disposed to move, speaking slowly, at first, and piece-
meal, alternating language with smoke, gradually
edged into the current of the evidence, and ended
by going all over it again, with fresh force and
point. His cigar glowed and chilled in the
darkening room as he talked.

" Now," he said, when he had drawn all the
threads together to the point of guilt, " what are
we going to do upon this evidence ?"

" I'll tell you something," said Eli. " I didn't
want to say it because I know what you'll all
think, but I'll tell you, all the same."

" Ah !" said the foreman.

Eli stood up and faced the others.

" 'Most all o' you know what our Bar is in a
south-east gale. They ain't a man here that 'uld
dare to try and cross it when the sea's breakin' on
it. The man that says he would, lies !" And he
looked at the foreman, and waited a moment.

" When my wife took sick, and I stopped goin'
to sea, two year ago, and took up boat-fishin', I
didn't know half as much about the coast as the

young boys do, and one afternoon it was blowin' a
gale, and we was all hands comin' in, and passin'
along the Bar to go sheer 'round it to the west'ard,
and Captain Fred Cook—he's short-sighted—got
on to the Bar before he knew it, and then he had
to go ahead, whether or no ; and I was right after
him, and I s'posed he knew, and I followed him.
Well, he was floated over, as luck was, all right ;
but when I'd just got on the Bar, a roller dropped
back and let my bowsprit down into the sand, and
then come up quicker'n lightnin' and shouldered
the boat over, t'other end first, and slung me into
the water ; and when I come up, I see somethin'
black, and there was John Wood's boat runnin' by
me before the wind with a rush—and 'fore I knew
an'thing he had me by the hair by one hand and in
his boat, and we was over the Bar.   Now, I tell
you, a man that looks the way I saw him look
when I come over the gunwale, face up, don't go
'round breakin' in and hookin' things.   He hadn't
one chance in five, and he was a married man, too,
with small children.   And what's more," he
added, incautiously, " he didn't stop there.   When
he found out, this last spring, that I was goin' to
lose my place, he lent me money enough to pay
the interest that was overdue on the mortgage, of
his own acord."

And he stopped suddenly.

" You have certainly explained yourself," said
the foreman.   " I think we understand you dis-
tinctly."

"There isn't one word of truth in that idea," said Eli, flushing up, "and you know it. I've paid him back every cent. I know him better'n any of you, that's all, and when I know he ain't guilty, I won't say he is ; and I can set here as long as any other man."

"Lively times some folks'll hev, when they go home," said a spare tin-peddler, stroking his long yellow goatee. "Go into the store : nobody speak to you ; go to cattle-show : everybody follow you 'round ; go to the wharf : nobody weigh your fish ; go to buy seed-cakes at the cart : baker won't give no tick."

"How much does it cost, Mr. Foreman," said the butcher, "for a man 't's obliged to leave town, to move a family out West ? I only ask for information. I have known a case where a man had to leave — couldn't live there no longer — wa'n't wanted."

There was a knock. An officer, sent by the judge, inquired whether the jury were likely soon to agree.

"It rests with you, sir," said the foreman, looking at Eli.

But Eli sat doggedly with his hands in his pockets, and did not look up or speak.

"Say to the judge that I cannot tell," said the foreman.

It was eight o'clock when the officer returned, with orders to take the jury across the street to the hotel, to supper. They went out in pairs, except

that the juryman who was left to fall in with Eli
made three with the file ahead, and left Eli to walk
alone. This was noticed by the by standers. At
the hotel, Eli could not eat a mouthful. He was
seated at one end of the table, and was left entirely
out of the conversation. When the jury were
escorted back to the court house, rumors had
evidently begun to arise from his having walked
alone, for there was quite a little crowd at the
hotel-door, to see them. They went as before :
four pairs, a file of three, and Eli alone. Then the
spectators understood it.

WHEN the jury were locked into their room again
for the night, Mr. Eldridge sat down by Eli, and
lit his pipe.

"I understand," he said, "just how you feel.
Now, between you and me, there was a good-
hearted fellow that kept me out of a bad mess once.
I've never told anybody just what it was, and I
don't mean to tell you now, but it brought my
blood up standing, to find how near I'd come to
putting a fine steamer and two hundred and forty
passengers under water. Well, one day, a year or
so after that, this man had a chance to get a good
ship, only there was some talk against him, that
he drank a little. Well, the owners told him they
wanted to see me, and he come to me, and says he,
'Mr. Eldridge, I hope you'll speak a good word
for me ; if you do, I'll get the ship, but if they
refuse me this one, I'm dished everywhere.' Well,

the owners put me the square question, and I had to tell 'em. Well, I met him that afternoon on Sacramento Street, as white as a sheet, and he wouldn't speak to me, but passed right by, and that night he went and shipped before the mast. That's the last I ever heard of him. But I had to do it.

" Now," he added, " this man's been good to you ; but the case is proved, and you ought to vote with the rest of us."

" It ain't proved," said Eli. " The judge said that if any man had a reasonable doubt, he ought to hold out. Now, I ain't convinced."

" Well, that's easy said," replied Mr. Eldridge, a little hotly, and he arose, and left him.

The jurymen broke up into little knots, tilted their chairs back, and settled into the easiest positions that their cramped quarters allowed. Most of them lit their pipes ; the captain, and one or two whom he honored, smoked fragrant cigars, and the room was soon filled with a dense cloud.

Eli sat alone by the window.

" Sometimes sell two at one house," said a lank book-agent, arousing himself from a reverie ; " once sold three."

" I think the Early Rose is about as profitable as any," said a little farmer, with a large circular beard. " I used to favor Jacobs's Seedling, but they haven't done so well with me of late years."

" Sometimes," said the book-agent, picking his teeth with a quill, " you'll go to a house, and they'll say they can't be induced to buy a book of

any kind, historical, fictitious, or religious ; but
you just keep on talking, and show the pictures—
' Grant in Boyhood,' ' Grant a Tanner,' ' Grant at
Head-quarters,' ' Grant in the White House,'
' Grant before Queen Victoria,' and they warm up,
I tell you, and not infrequently buy."

" Do you sell de ' Illustrated Bible,' " asked
Washington, " wid de Hypocrypha ?"

" No ; I have a more popular treatise—the
' Illustrated History of the Bible.' Greater
variety. Brings in the surrounding nations, in
costume. Cloth, three dollars ; sheep, three-fifty ;
half calf, five-seventy-five, full morocco, gilt edges,
seven-fifty. Six hundred and seven illustrations
on wood and steel. Three different engravings of
Abraham alone. Four of Noah—' Noah before the
Flood,' ' Noah Building the Ark,' ' Noah Wel-
coming the Dove,' ' Noah on Ararat.' Steel engraving of Ezekiel's Wheel, explaining prophecy.
Jonah under the gourd, Nineveh in the distance."

Mr. Eldridge and Captain Thomas had drifted
into a discussion of harbors, and the captain had
drawn his chair up to the table, and, with a cigar
in his mouth, was explaining an ingeniously con-
structed foreign harbor. He was making a rough
sketch, with a pen.

" Here is north," he said ; " here is the coast-
line ; here are the flats ; here are the sluice-gates ;
they store the water here, in——"

Some of the younger men had their heads together, in a corner, about the tin-peddler, who was

telling stories of people he had met in his journeys, which brought out repeated bursts of laughter.

In the corner farthest from Eli, a delicate-looking man began to tell the butcher about Eli's wife.

" Twelve years ago this fall," he said, " I taught district-school in the parish where she lived. She was about fourteen then. Her father was a poor farmer, without any faculty. Her mother was dead, and she kept house. I stayed there one week, boarding 'round."

" Prob'ly didn't git not much of any fresh meat that week," suggested the butcher.

" She never said much, but it used to divert me to see her order around her big brothers, just as if she was their mother. She and I got to be great friends ; but she was a queer piece. One day at school, the girls in her row were communicating, and annoying me, while the third class was reciting in ' First Steps in Numbers,' and I was so incensed that I called Lizzie—that's her name—right out, and had her stand up for twenty minutes. She was a shy little thing, and set great store by perfect marks. I saw that she was troubled a good deal, to have all of them looking and laughing at her. But she stood there, with her hands folded behind her, and not a smile or a word."

" Look out for a sullen cow," said the butcher.

" I felt afraid I had been too hasty with her, and I was rather sorry I had been so decided—although, to be sure, she didn't pretend to deny that she had been communicating."

" Of course," said the butcher : " no use lyin' when you're caught in the act."

" Well, after school, she stayed at her desk, fixing her dinner-pail, and putting her books in a strap, and all that, till all the rest had gone, and then she came up to my desk, where I was correcting compositions."

" Now for music !" said the butcher.

" She had been crying a little. Well, she looked straight in my face, and said she, ' Mr. Pollard, I just wanted to say to you that I wasn't doing any-thing at all when you called me up ;' and off she went. Now, that was just like her—too proud to say a word before the school."

But here his listener's attention was diverted by the voice of the book-agent :

" The very best Bible for teachers, of course, is the limp-cover, protected edges, full Levant morocco, Oxford, silk-sewed, kid-lined, Bishop's Divinity Circuit, with concordance, maps of the Holy Land, weights, measures, and money-tables of the Jews. Nothing like having a really——"

" And so," said the captain, moving back his chair, " they let on the whole head of water, and scour out the channel to a T."

And then he rapped upon the table.

" Gentlemen," he said, " please draw your chairs up, and let us take another ballot."

The count resulted as before. The foreman muttered something which had a scriptural sound.

In a few moments, he drew Mr. Eldridge and two

others aside. " Gentlemen," he said to them, " I shall quietly divide the jury into watches, under your charge : ten can sleep, while one wakes to keep Mr. Smith discussing the question. I don't propose to have the night wasted."

And, by one man or another, Eli was kept awake.

" I DON'T see," said the book-agent, " why you should feel obliged to stick it out any longer. Of course, you are under obligations. But you've done more than enough already, so as that he can't complain of you, and if you give in now, everybody'll give you credit for trying to save your friend, on the one hand, and, on the other hand, for giving in to the evidence. So you'll get credit both ways."

An hour later, the tin-peddler came on duty. He had not followed closely the story about John Wood's loan, and had got it a little awry.

" Now, how foolish you be," he said, in a confidential tone. " Can't you see that if you cave in now, after stan'n' out nine hours"—and he looked at a silver watch with a brass chain, and stroked his goatee — " nine hours and twenty-seven minutes—that you've made jest rumpus enough so as't he won't dare to foreclose on you, for fear they'll say you went back on a trade. On t'other hand, if you hold clear out, he'll turn you out-o'-doors to-morrow, for a blind, so 's to look as if there wa'n't no trade between you. Once he gits

off, he won't know Joseph, you bet ! That's what
I'd do," he added, with a sly laugh. " Take your
uncle's advice."

" The only trouble with that," said Eli, shortly,
" is that I don't owe him anything."

" Oh," said the peddler ; " that makes a difference. I understood you did."

Three o'clock came, and brought Mr. Eldridge.
He found Eli worn out with excitement.

" Now I don't judge you the way the others
do," said Mr. Eldridge, in a low tone, with his
hand on Eli's knee. " I know, as I told you, just
the way you feel. But we can't help such things.
Suppose, now, that I had kept dark, and allowed
to the owners that that man was always sober, and
I had heard, six months after, of thirty or forty
men going to the bottom because the captain was
a little off his base ; and then to think of their
wives and children at home. We have to do some
hard things ; but I say, do the square thing, and
let her slide."

" But I can't believe he's guilty," said Eli.

" But don't you allow," said Mr. Eldridge,
" that eleven men are more sure to hit it right than
one man ?"

" Yes," said Eli, reluctantly, " as a general
thing."

" Well, there's always got to be some give to a
jury, just as in everything else, and you ought to
lay right down on the rest of us. It isn't as if we
were at all squirmish. Now, you know that if you
hold out, he'll be tried again."

" Yes, I suppose so."

" Got to be—no other way," said Mr. Eldridge.
" Now, the next time, there won't be anybody like
you to stand out, and the judge'll know of this
scrape, and he'll just sock it to him."

Eli turned uneasily in his chair.

" And then it won't be understood in your place,
and folks'll turn against you every way, and,
what's worse, let you alone."

" I can stand it," said Eli, angrily. " Let 'em
do as they like. They can't kill me."

" They can kill your wife and break down your
children," said Mr. Eldridge. " Women and
children can't stand it. Now there's that man
they were speaking of ; he lived down my way.
He sued a poor, shiftless fellow that had come
from Pennsylvania to his daughter's funeral, and
had him arrested and taken off, crying, just before
the funeral begun—after they'd even set the
flowers on the coffin ; and nobody'd speak to him
after that—they just let him alone ; and after a
while his wife took sick of it—she was a nice,
kindly woman—and she had sort of hysterics, and,
finally, he moved off West. And 'twasn't long
before the woman died. Now, you can't under-
take to do different from everybody else."

" Well," said Eli ; " I know I wish it was done
with."

Mr. Eldridge stretched his arms and yawned.
Then he began to walk up and down, and hum,
out of tune. Then he stopped at Captain Thomas's
chair.

"Suppose we try a ballot," he said. "He seems to give a little."

In a moment the foreman rapped.

"It is time we were taking another ballot, gentlemen," he said.

The sleepers rose, grumbling, from uneasy dreams.

"I will write 'guilty' on twelve ballots," said the foreman, "and if any one desires to write in 'not,' of course he can."

When the hat came to Eli, he took one of the ballots and held it in his hand a moment ; and then he laid it on the table. There was a general murmur. The picture which Mr. Eldridge had drawn loomed up before him. But with a hasty hand he wrote in "not," dropped in the ballot, and going back to his chair by the window, sat down.

There was a cold wave of silence.

Then Eli suddenly walked up to the foreman and faced him.

"Now," he said, "we'll stop. The very next turn breaks ground. If you, or any other man that you set on, tries to talk to me when I don't want to hear, to worry me to death—look out !"

How the long hours wore on ! How easy, sometimes, to resist an open pressure, and how hard, with the resistance gone, to fight, as one that beats the air ! How the prospect of a whole hostile town loomed up, in a mirage, before Eli ! And then the picture rose before him of a long, stately bark, now building, whose owner had asked him yesterday to be first mate. And if his wife were only well, and he were only free from this night's trouble, how soon, upon the long, green waves, he could begin to redeem his little home !

And then came Mr. Eldridge, kind and friendly, to have another little chat.

MORNING came, cold and drizzly. An officer knocked at the door, and called out, "Breakfast." And, in a moment, unwashed, and all uncombed, except the tin-peddler, who always carried a beard-comb in his pocket, they were marched across the street to the hotel.

There were a number of men on the piazza waiting to see them — jurymen, witnesses, and the accused himself, for he was on bail. He had seen the procession the night before, and, like the others, had read its meaning.

"Eli knows I wouldn't do it," he had said to himself, "and he's going to hang out, sure."

The jury began to turn from the court-house door. Everybody looked. A file of two men, another file, another, another ; would there come three men, and then one ? No ; Eli no longer walked alone.

Everybody looked at Wood ; he turned sharply away.

But this time the order of march in fact showed nothing, one way or the other. It only meant that the judge, who had happened to see the jury the night before returning from their supper, had sent for the high sheriff in some temper—for judges are human—and had vigorously intimated that if that statesman did not look after his fool of a deputy, who let a jury parade secrets to the public view, he would——!

THE jury were in their room again. At nine o'clock came a rap, and a summons from the court.

The prosecuting attorney was speaking with the judge when they went in. In a moment he took his seat.

"John Wood !" called out the clerk, and the defendant arose. His attorney was not there.

"Mr. Foreman !" said the judge, rising. The jury arose. The silence of the crowded court-room was intense.

"Before the clerk asks you for a verdict, gentlemen," said the judge, "I have something of the first importance to say to you, which has but this moment come to my knowledge."

Eli changed color, and the whole court-room looked at him.

"There were some most singular rumors, after the case was given to you, gentlemen, to the effect that there had been in this cause a criminal abuse of justice. It is painful to suspect, and shocking to know, that courts and juries are liable ever to suffer by such unprincipled practices. After ten years upon the bench, I never witness a conviction of crime without pain ; but that pain is light, compared with the distress of knowing of a wilful per-

version of justice. It is a relief to me to be able
to say to you that such instances are, in my judgment, exceedingly rare, and—so keen is the awful
searching power of truth—are almost invariably
discovered.''

The foreman touched his neighbor with his
elbow. Eli folded his arms.

'' As I said,'' continued the judge, '' there were
most singular rumors. During the evening and
the night, rumor, as is often the case, led to
evidence, and evidence has led to confession and
to certainty. And the district attorney now desires me to say to you that the chief officer of the
bank—who held the second key to the safe—is now
under arrest for a heavy defalcation, which a sham
robbery was to conceal, and that you may find the
prisoner at the bar—not guilty. I congratulate
you, gentlemen, that you had not rendered an
adverse verdict.''

'' Your Honor !'' said Eli ; and he cleared his
throat ; '' I desire it to be known that, even as the
case stood last night, this jury had not agreed to
convict, and never would have !''

There was a hush, while a loud scratching pen
indorsed the record of acquittal. Then Wood
walked down to the jury-box and took Eli's hand.

'' Just what I told my wife all through,'' he
said. '' I knew you'd hang out !''

Eli's jury was excused for the rest of the day,
and by noon he was in his own village, relieved,

too, of his most pressing burden : for George
Cahoon had met him on the road, and told him
that he was not going to the West, after all, for the
present, and should not need his money.   But, as
he turned the bend of the road and neared his
house, he felt a rising fear that some disturbing
rumor might have reached his wife about his action
on the jury.   And, to his distress and amazement,
there she was, sitting in a chair at the door.

"Lizzie !" he said, "what does this mean ?
Are you crazy ?"

"I'll tell you what it means," she said, as she
stood up with a little smile and clasped her hands
behind her.   "This morning, it got around and
came to me that you was standing out all alone for
John Wood, and that the talk was that they'd be
down on you, and drive you out of town, and that
everybody pitied *me—pitied me !*   And when I heard
that, I thought I'd see !   And my strength seemed
to come all back, and I got right up, and dressed
myself.   And what's more, I'm going to get well
now !"

And she did.

YOUNG STRONG OF "THE CLARION."

BY MILICENT WASHBURN SHINN.

IF you had asked any resident of Green's Ferry some eight years ago—say, in '76—who were the leading men of his town, he would doubtless have begun :

" Well, there's Judge Garvey, of course. Then there's Uncle Billy Green, who built the first shanty there in '49, and young Strong of ' The Clarion '—"

However he might continue his enumeration, it would certainly have been as above for the first three names. One you would have recognized, if you had been following State politics closely for some years ; for Judge Garvey was very regularly chosen State senator in his district, and had held the barren honor of presidential elector the last time his party carried the State. In '76, some of the papers were urging his nomination for Con-

** *Overland Monthly, September*, 1884.

gress, and politicians thought his chance of such a nomination increasing. It has not turned out so ; his name has quite dropped out of the papers, and it is said he does not certainly control his own county now ; but at that time he was the most potent political influence in three counties. What he influenced them to, I never clearly understood, for I cannot recall that I ever heard his name mentioned in connection with any measure or opinion.

A file of " The Clarion" during the four years that young Strong was editor would doubtless throw light on the matter. " The Clarion" was at this time a sort of voice crying in the wilderness about Reform, which was a very new idea, indeed, to its readers. Garvey did not like the paper, and young Strong disliked Garvey very much ; but the two men had kept on fairly good terms—not so rigid good terms, of course, as to forbid their expressing to third parties the frankest contempt for each other. The Judge had here the advantage, for Strong despised him indignantly, as a knave, while he despised Strong—or said he did—pityingly, as a fool. He must, however, have at bottom honored the young fellow with some serious antipathy ; for it was after all no laughing matter that a boy of twenty-five should come into " his Gaul, which he had conquered by arms," and filch away his home paper from under his very eyes. Moreover, though people read the editorials, laughed, and voted with the Judge just the same—they still did read them. However,

Judge Garvey certainly was more civil to Strong
than Strong was to him.

As for Uncle Billy Green, his rank was due not
only to his connection with the " first shanty" (a
house of entertainment at the point where a trail
turned from the river toward the mines), but to his
having remained steadily on the .spot ever since,
putting up a larger building at intervals as the set-
tlement gathered around him, until now he was
proprietor of the American Eagle Hotel, a house of
goodly dimensions and generous equipment—bill-
iard-room, bowling alley, shooting-gallery. Nor
did Uncle Billy Green own and conduct this house
in a purely business spirit ; a more modest one
would have been more profitable ; he liked to " do
that much for the town." A man by the name of
Gulliver had established the old rope-ferry, before
the day of bridges, but it was naturally called
Green's Ferry, being a ferry at Green's place. He
had been of an undoubted valor in the Indian
fights of early days, was full of reminiscences, had
no personal objections to anybody or anything,
and had long given over to Judge Garvey the
trouble of forming his opinions.

Judge Garvey and young Strong were pretty
sure to be put upon such boards or committees as
the local affairs of the small town demanded ; and
in local matters they proved to pull together fairly
well, however at odds they were politically. But
in the end it was not over politics, but over the
district school, that they fell out squarely. They

were both trustees, and as Green was the third, the board seemed in little danger from any too radical reforming tendencies young Strong might be guilty of, and the Judge had no thought of danger as he walked down to " The Clarion" office, a breathless September afternoon, a couple of days before the school should open.

He found young Strong in his editorial room. This was a corner of the printing-office, fenced off by a great screen pasted over with old exchanges. Behind this, Strong sat at his table, correcting proof energetically. It was evident that he took the editing of this little four-page weekly rather seriously—but, then, a man must needs be business-like to produce even four pages weekly with one assistant, and Strong had to economize time enough from strictly editorial functions to do a goodly share of type-setting and the rest of the mechanics of the office.

" I beg your pardon for interrupting you, Mr. Strong," said the Judge. " I perceive you are arduously occupied. But it becomes necessary to confer with you with regard to the school-teacher."

The Judge was a tall and vigorously built man—a little red-faced, but good-looking, if one did not insist on too fine a definiteness of outline. He spoke habitually with a certain inflation of manner, and tried to form himself upon a Southern type that was pretty abundant in our politics some years earlier. He was, however, a native of rural New York, early transplanted to California.

Strong turned in his chair, and sitting sidewise, rested his elbow on the proof-sheets, holding the pencil still in his fingers.

"Well?" he said. "I thought everything was settled."

"Assuredly." Judge Garvey rested his folded arms upon the pile of books stacked at the rear of the table, and leaned over them in a friendly way. "Mr. Coakley is to arrive Sunday evening, and will begin the term on Monday morning, to the great satisfaction, I can guarantee, of all concerned. A slight and merely temporary embarrassment has arisen, with respect to which a few words will make it all right. In point of fact, the young woman with whom we previously held correspondence—who, you will remember, broke her engagement with us to take a more advantageous position—is here."

The Judge stopped for question or comment, but as Strong waited for explanation, he went on :

"She has, it appears, failed after all to secure that, and come here expecting to fall back upon our school, not having heard that it was engaged."

"Well, that's unfortunate for her," said Strong, "but you can't ship Coakley now."

"Your views coincide exactly with my own, my dear sir." The Judge straightened up with some relief. "I have only to ask, then, for a note to the lady to that effect, that my own explanation already given may be corroborated."

Strong began to look alert and suspicious at this.

" Views coincide ?" he said. " What two views could there be ? What does she say brought her here ?"

" She's got an idea that she's got first claim on the place," said the Judge, plumping suddenly into colloquial diction. He had a trick of doing so when he got down to business. It would have had something the effect of candid confession, produced by a maiden's plain-hair days alternated with her waved-hair days, had not the grandiloquence of tone and manner become so far second nature that it ran through both his dialects, and lessened the contrast. " You can't always make a woman see sense."

Strong looked suspiciously at him a few seconds. " Well, I'll go see her this evening," he said. " Where's she staying ?"

" That is a totally superfluous tax on your time, my dear Strong," said the Judge, leaning persuasively across the books again. " I have here a mere formal line, stating that Coakley is the regularly engaged teacher of the school, and will begin next Monday ; your signature to it—Green's and mine are already there—will be all that is necessary." He pushed pen and ink toward Strong with his exaggerated air of courtesy.

" Oh, I'm not going to sign things that way, you know. I'll go see her." He turned and drew his proof-sheets to him with an air of dismissal.

The Judge stood up very straight, expanded his chest, and folded his arms according to his con-

ception of the Virginian manner. "Am I to understand, sir, that you question my veracity?"

"I don't question anything," said the young
man, impatiently. "I'll know what I'm talking
about when I've seen her."

"Permit me to suggest, sir"—the Judge was
approaching his platform manner—"permit me
to suggest, sir, that Mr. Green and myself consti-
tute a majority of the board, and Mr. Green, sir—
Uncle Billy Green—has confidence in my honor,
and will sustain my action, whatever line *you* may
be persuaded to adopt."

"Oh, as to that," said Strong, exaggerating his
crispness of manner in protest against the Judge's
staginess, "I'm clerk of the board, and you can't
hold a legal meeting nor pay a salary without me.
What's the reason you don't want me to see her?"

Judge Garvey unfolded his arms, fell back a
step, and dropped easily into the sonorous decla-
mation that made the stalwart Judge no inconspic-
uous figure on the floor of the Legislature. The
newspapers, of course, were responsible for his
language—as for the rest of his education; but
such as it was, he used it fluently, and the decla-
matory manner was, to his constituency, quite an
essential of eloquence—the prime difference, in
fact, between oratory and plain talking.

"You cast aspersions upon my honor, sir.
Through me you insult the people of Green's
Ferry—of this county—of this district—the en-
lightened and honorable constituency who it is my

proud honor to represent. I sco-r-n to answer
your insinuations, sir. They will be hurled back
upon yourself by the united voice and righteous
indignation of my justly aroused fellŏw-townsmen,
by the voters of this noble district—I may say, by
the whole State of California—to which I am not
unknown, sir.''

Half-a-dozen of the justly aroused fellow-townsmen were straggling in from the street, for in
Green's Ferry a sprinkling of the citizens spend
the warm afternoons sitting in absolute tranquillity
on boxes and barrels here and there, under the
awnings of the several business blocks ; and the
knowledge that a row was at last on between Judge
Garvey and young Strong reached them at the
first peal. The Judge, alive to the increase of his
audience, raised his voice a shade, and went on
with a curious mixture of complacency and genuine wrath.

" Is it lack of confidence that has sent me to
represent my honorable constituency in the legisla-
tive halls of California, Mr. Strong ? Have I received that proud token of esteem only to be insulted by one whose obscurity is his only shield ;
who, with unknown record, with no recommenda-
tion save his own overwhelming self-esteem, comes
among us to sow dissent in peaceful counsels, and
draw scorn and contempt upon his own head by
impotent and futile attacks upon those whom he is
powerless to harm ?''

This rounded the climax well, so the Judge only

added : " The call you propose, sir, I shall regard as a direct insult to myself," and strode dramatically from the room.

The papered screen went crashing to the floor behind him. The justly aroused fellow-townsmen looked after him, laughing but admiring.

" Laid you out, didn't he, Strong ?"

" That's the way he does it at Sacramento. Oh, the Judge is a real orator—there's no doubt of that."

"*He* don't have to make his speech up beforehand. No, sir, right where he is, any time of day, he just turns the faucet, and there it comes."

" What was the row, anyway, Strong ?"

" I don't know myself ; something about a teacher—he began to bluster all of a sudden." Strong walked over to the screen, picked it up, set it straight along a crack with intense precision, and went back to his seat. " Drunk, isn't he ? I haven't heard him take the stump that way since election. He's always made rather a point of not quarrelling with me, too."

" Oh, he's no drunker'n usual," answered with candor a fellow-townsman. " The Judge ain't really himself until he's a little off. He didn't blow so without some reason ; don't you fool yourself—not if *I* know the man."

" Well, if he's got any game he must have come to his last chance in it, to try bullying on *me*," said Strong ; and then another of the group asked :

"What row could there be about a teacher, Strong? Thought you'd given him his man."

The pencil rolled from the edge of the table across the floor at Strong's movement of attention. "Coakley?—what of him?"

The man began to laugh, and one or two others joined in. One of them said a little offensively: "Pretty good on you, youngster! You took too big a contract for your age when you undertook to keep up with Judge Garvey. He'll give you odds and take you in, every time."

Strong reddened a little, but waited to be answered with very fair composure.

"Didn't you really know, Strong? The Judge scored one on you that time, then. Why, he's been Garvey's man in Sierra Township one or two elections now. Used to be a Millerite preacher, before your day, but he broke down at that. Good hand in county politics, but he's always completely out of business between times. Why you remember him, Strong—he was round with the Judge election times — cross-eyed fellow, with black siders."

"*That* fellow? Why, he can't spell straight! The way of it was, Judge Garvey told us only Tuesday that the teacher we'd got—first-rate certificates—had backed out ; and we couldn't put off beginning school any longer, nor hear of any teacher to be had ; so when he produced this man, we had really no choice. I suppose I needn't ask where he got his certificates."

" No—Garvey's solid with this county board
and superintendent."

" Disgraceful !" said Strong ; whereat all
laughed, except one who had lost a ranch a few
years before during business dealings with the
Judge.

" Oh, he's a scamp—I wouldn't trust him out of
sight with his baby's silver mug," said this man,
with feeling. The rest laughed again. In Green's
Ferry a certain easy-going good-heartedness is re-
quired by the public conscience, rather than deca-
logue virtues. Garvey liked sharp practice—all
right ; if you were yourself hurt, you would naturally begin to vote against him ; otherwise, it was
none of your business, except as successful rascal-
ity had a claim on your admiration. Young
Strong liked to write furious reform editorials—all
right ; if you were the one hit, you would swear at
Strong and stop your subscription until a hit on
some one else made you renew it ; otherwise, it
was none of your business and lively reading.
They leaned against the wall and desk, and began
with perfect good-nature to tell stories of the
Judge. " R'member the time he got that Mexican
ranch ? Fellow thought it was a bill of sale for
thirty acres he was signing, and it was three hundred."

" Best thing was when he made old man Meeker
believe he was dying, and deed over a good fifty
thousand dollars in stock to his daughter—and
married the girl, sir, before the old fellow found

he was good for twenty years more. He made the
air smell of brimstone the rest of his life if you
mentioned Garvey to him ! Drowned in a ford a
winter or two later, after all. Used to live in a
little shanty up Indian Crick and raise potatoes—
and Garvey sent him a cow—cheekiest thing !"

Strong turned sharply away from the laugh that
followed, and went on with his work, while they
slowly dispersed. He worked on savagely with
brows drawn together. "It isn't so much the existence of scoundrels like Garvey that gets me," he
was saying to himself, "as the way the whole
crowd of them take him." He stopped to read
over the words he was correcting—they were editorial :

"Was ever folly greater than this of our com-
munity, in dropping everything else to run after
money. For what do you expect to do with it
when you get it ? Better eating, and drinking,
and the privilege of being toadied to ·by those who
want to make something out of you—what more
can you get out of money, if you have never made
anything of *yourself ?* Just as a pig, if he might
take his choice whether he would be turned into a
man or would be moved into a cosier sty, with
more unbounded swill, would doubtless choose the
sty !"

"My broom against the ocean," he said ; but he
went on correcting doggedly.

And, not to conceal from you what was in reality
the most significant fact about Will Strong—the

key to about everything he thought and did—he
was mentally submitting this editorial, as he had
submitted every other he had written, to the test
of the probable opinion of a young woman he had
not seen nor heard from for two years, but who
nevertheless constituted to his mind the chief mo-
tive for existence—if not the chief and sufficient
explanation of the human race's having been cre-
ated at all. You must realize, before trying to understand his story, that Will Strong was really a
very romantic young man indeed, though he pre-
tended to Green's Ferry that he was not.

Outside the screen, the strips of sun through the
western window and open door lengthened across
the meagre collection of dusty fonts of type, the
small press, the piles of papers. The black-fin-
gered, red-haired boy setting type among them
reflected that it must be nearly dinner-time, and
turned to see how far in the hot strips had crept—
turned, and stood staring ; for he met squarely the
inquiring look of a pair of clear eyes, and became
aware of a lady in the doorway.

It is probable that Jim had never dreamed in his
life of any other social distinction than that between rich and poor, notorious and obscure, nor
was he a lad of perceptions ; yet he knew at once
that this was a very unusual sort of lady for
Green's Ferry. If he had been a man of the social
world he would have known that she was a gentle-
woman of notably high-bred appearance. She
glanced, not without dismay, about the shabby

work-room, as if she felt herself where she had no business to be. Nevertheless, she came forward frankly, and asked in the friendly way of one whose station needs no asserting :

" Mr. Strong ?—one of the school-board ?—Is he here ?"

" Yes'm." The boy made no motion, but stood blankly staring.

" May I see him, please ?"

" Lady to see you, Mr. Strong," shouted Jim, standing still.

In the few seconds before Strong emerged, the lady stood her ground in the middle of the floor, with some appearance of anxiety. She was certainly a very noticeable person, and came nearer to warranting that strong word " beautiful " than falls often to the lot of woman. It was a matter of outline more than color, however, for she had not much of that about her—brown hair, blue-gray eyes, skin of a warm paleness. All this low coloring, however, was so perfect of its sort, that it gave something the effect of a fine etching—a rich distinctness attained by shades, not colors. Instead of being outshone by more brilliant-hued women, Miss Northrop had always had the effect of making them look chromo-like. So, too, a certain nobility and self-forgetfulness of manner made the more elaborate manners of others seem the crude device of inferiority. It was a good deal due to her eyes ; she had most wonderful eyes, and I doubt if any man or many women ever met them in a full look without feeling a little stir of pulse—whether it was in the lashes, or in the sweet straightforwardness of look, utterly devoid of coquetry, or in the depth of the gray, or in what ; certain it is that no one ever saw Miss Northrop without talking of her beautiful eyes.

" A lady to see him ?" The word in Green's Ferry defined only the sex. Some one with a notice of a flock of sheep for sale, which she wanted to get in as a local ; or with an ill-spelled poem ; or—by George, yes—that school-mistress. Lucky she had not met Garvey there—poor girl ! Strong laid his pencil down, and came out from behind the screen good-naturedly enough—and stopped short. What a thing to happen to a man, that he should live and move and have his being for a dozen years in the thought of one woman, should count a world worth living in because she was somewhere on it, and a pitiful human race worth working for because they were her fellow-creatures—and should come out from behind his screen, and see her before his eyes—on his dingy workroom floor—out of her four thousand miles' distance !

They had been four years schoolmates in a New England High School. Will was a farmer's lad, from an outlying, rocky village, who worked for his board while he went to school. He came of an unschooled, hard-working, God-fearing yeoman race. Winifred could look up every line of her descent, through vista of governors, college-presidents, and ministers, back to Colonial aristocracy and gentry beyond sea. Her great-grandfathers had carried swords in Revolutionary battles, where Will's had followed with muskets. Winifred herself was one of those flowers into which excellent family trees break occasionally—flowers so lovely that no excellence of the tree seems enough to account for them. If she had any core of aristocratic coldness, it was so overlaid by a sweet humaneness, a frank generosity of impulse, that no one would have known it. If she had been a man, to have a valet, she would have been a hero to him.

Even in the democracy of school, Will Strong knew well enough the difference between his shy awkwardness and her pleasant frankness; and knew that though he could meet school requirements about as well as she, yet his mental range was crude and narrow beside hers; and any one could see that in the town where he was an unknown boy she was an important young lady. These things would not have counted for much had not some mediæval follower of some exiled king dropped down into the boy's temperament that passion of self-abasing loyalty that is rather an anachronism in our democratic days. They had been on terms of friendliness rather than friendship in school, but that was due more to his shyness than anything else. She had really given to him more opportunities than to most of her schoolmates; she liked his integrity and earnestness.

He had looked to college as the natural door between his world and hers ; after four years at New Haven he might seek her acquaintance without audacity. To that end he had laboriously accumulated money, and had even passed his matriculation, when his father's death made him indispensable on the poor little farm. Since then he had doggedly plodded alone through the college curriculum, but without finding in it the mysterious pass-word that he had expected into the intellectual aristocracy. Some two years before, his mother's death and the growing up of younger brothers had left him free to seek his fortune in California. At twenty-seven he had lost his fresh look and boyish shyness ; he looked older than he was, but he was really very youthful, and believed in all sorts of abstractions beginning with capitals. His mental furniture, being obtained from books, not people, was not quite in the style of the present decade, and he read Carlyle and Emerson more than Herbert Spencer. His creed had, therefore, quite transcendentalism enough to accommodate without incongruity his little private deification.

Once in every year or two, as opportunity took him near her home, he had called on her, and had multiplied each call mightily by thinking of it before and after. He had also kept up a stupid correspondence with a schoolmate who had lived in the same town with her, for the chance of her name being mentioned. Within a couple of years, however, she had lost her father and gone to relatives

in New York, so he had lost exact knowledge even
of her whereabouts.

She spoke before he had found his voice—without an instant's hesitation, indeed. " Oh, Will
Strong !" she cried, stepping quickly toward him
and holding out her hand. " I *hoped* it was you !"

He took the offered hand, and said to himself that
his own was consecrated by the touch to clean
deeds forever. He would not have known how to
address her, but he followed her leading.

" It is Winifred Northrop !" he said. " What is
it ? Can I do something for you ?"

" You are school-committee man, are you not ?"
Anxiety, relief, and trust mingled in her voice.

" Trustee—yes. Why," he cried, " it isn't possible that *you* are the lady !"

She laughed. " I suppose the lady must be I."

He did not smile. He even lost color with
wrath. " Garvey has dared to play you some
trick !—I did not dream—" he went on, eagerly,
" Garvey kept the letters in his hands, and bungled
over the name, so I did not once fairly catch it."

He turned back to his corner, and put the remaining bit of proof into his pocket. New heavens
and new earth had come into existence since the
last pencil mark on it.

" Jim," he said, " I'm called off on school-busi-
ness. You get as much of that set up as you can
before dinner, and then lock up ; and I'll come
down and make the corrections in the editorials
before I go to bed. Now—Winifred—if I may

walk home with you, we'll get to the bottom of
Garvey's tricks. Villain !"'

The epithet was so fervent, and so entirely without humorous intent, that Miss Northrop laughed
again as they walked out into the dull, hot September afternoon sun. The board sidewalk was
uneven and full of projecting nails and splinters,
and she held her thin, blue-gray dress prettily
aside from them ; Will noted the gesture with admiration as intense as unreasonable. It seemed to
him peculiarly admirable that she should draw her
hat a little forward to shade her eyes, and should
take just the length of step that she did ; the absolutely right step for a lady was thenceforth settled ; since then, he has insisted unreasonably
upon a certain shade as the only right thing in
gray, as if he held in his own mind some positive
standard beyond the realm of variable taste.

The two or three business blocks—rows of slight
frame-buildings, more of them saloons than would
seem possible—were very quiet ; Green's Ferry is
the shipping point of a wide stock-raising district,
and all its activity centres about the railroad station at stated times daily. The justly aroused fellow-townsmen were all back under the awnings—
leaning against the wall by the post-office, sitting
on boxes by the grocery ; some indolently telling
stories and chaffing ; some looking sleepily before
them in absolute repose ; some in various stages of
inert drunkenness. All stared curiously at young
Strong and the strange lady, and prepared to

talk them over afterward, but no one addressed him.

They turned aside soon into a broad cross street with no sidewalk, where the coarse dust was in places ankle deep. Behind them, beyond the main street, a few groups of yellowing cottonwoods on bare banks of reddish clay marked the course of the Sacramento ; before them the street faded into a limitless expanse of gravel, thinly dotted in the distance with dull green oaks, and bounded by long knolls, like wrinkles in the plain, dark with oaks against the smoky sky of September—a sky dull blue above, dull gray near the horizon.

Along either side of the street the flimsy wooden houses were set back, each in its yard, and surrounded by oleanders ; sometimes there would be, a few parched roses, a trellis of Madeira-vine, a patch of carefully nursed grass, often a row of China trees, whose fallen black seeds stippled the dust—but always the great rosy clumps of oleanders, glorying in the heat and drought. Every evening after dinner the owners come out, and stand watering these gardens with hose and sprinkler, till all along the street there is a murmur like rain and a smell of damp earth, and here and there through the warm twilight a glimpse of the white sprays of water ; while the families sit on the porches and doorstep, and gossip and laugh. At this hour, however, the little gardens and splendid oleanders lay hot and deserted in the dusty afternoon.

" I haven't till now had time to spare from being anxious to be interested," Miss Northrop said.
" I was rather panic-stricken this morning, and
things were awful, instead of interesting, in pro-
portion to their newness."

This bit of pathos stiffened Will's manner with
the awkwardness of over-feeling, as he asked :
" Now, what can I do for you—Winifred ?"

The awkwardness made him more like the
school-boy Will ; and then, a familiar face four
thousand miles from home seems more familiar
than it really is. Miss Northrop answered confid-
ingly : " I will tell you all about it, and then you
will know what to do. I wrote to Judge Garvey—
some one referred me to him at Sacramento—and
asked if I might teach the school. He wrote back
that I might, fixed the day, and directed me to a
boarding-place that he had engaged for me. So I
came by yesterday evening's train, and sent word
that I was here. This morning he called and told
me—with most oppressive civility—that as I had
not answered his last letter, the place had been
given to some one else. He said ' professional eti-
quette ' here demands an answer in such a case,
and failure to answer is equivalent to a withdrawal
of the application."

" He lied," said Will, parenthetically, walking
along with his eyes on the ground ; she, on the
contrary, looked at him often, with frank direct-
ness.

" He did not impress me," she said, " as the

soul of candor. I said as little as possible to him, but when he was gone I asked about the rest of the committee, and as soon as I heard your name I hoped it was you ; I knew you were somewhere in California. This afternoon I received his letter written to prevent my coming. It had followed me up here by the same train that I came on." She held the letter in her hand, and Will quietly took it and kept it. "I would not raise any controversy about such a thing," she went on, "if I had any idea in the world where else to go or what to do." Her voice sharpened a little again, with a note of pathos. .

Will did not know how to answer without seeming to question or comment, so there came a pause ; then he said :

"This Coakley was an electioneering agent of Garvey's, and doesn't know enough to teach babies. He seems to have turned up suddenly wanting help, and the Judge is willing enough to keep him on hand and under obligations until next election."

Miss Northrop stopped short and looked at him with brows a little raised, and her bearing became impalpably more distant.

"But I cannot enter into contest with—these men for permission to teach school here," she said.

She was right, in her quick feeling that Will Strong's training could not have made work and discomfort and contact with vulgarity seem outside the sphere of women. If it had been one of his own sisters he would have said : " Oh, well, we have to take the world as we find it. ˙Brace up, little girl ; I'll put you safe through, and you'll find it's not so bad, after all."

But what he said to Winifred Northrop was : " It is outrageous ! Such brutes as Garvey have no business to look at a lady ! If you really prefer not to take the school," he went on, with some embarrassment, " I hope you will call on me to help you in any other way ; but if you want the school you shall have it, and no annoyance with it that I can help."

Miss Northrop repented that she had repented her confidence. " I remembered that you were kind of old, Will "—and her manner was irresistibly winning when she said such a thing—" but you are so very kind now that you make me ashamed. I only meant to ask you what I must do. Yes, I must take this position if I can, for I have no alternative."

" There is nothing for you to do," he said. " It is my place, as an officer of the school, to see that its rightful teacher is not defrauded."

" So it is," she said, relieved. " But I am none the less grateful."

" It is a pleasure to me to be able to do anything for you," he said, gravely, somewhat stiffly—from his tone you would not have suspected much more truth than usual in the formula.

She only said : " You are very kind," and then he lifted his hat, and left her at Mrs. Stutt's gate.

He deliberately and literally believed, as he

walked down the street—directly to Green's—that
he was the happiest man in the world. For that
matter, it is not impossible that he was. He was
absolutely innocent of conscious hyperbole in saying, " It would be worth a life-time of trouble only
to have *seen* her ; and I know her and am able to
do her a service !"

He scored one advantage in having seen Miss
Northrop early ; he saw Green before Garvey had
talked with him. The report of the quarrel had
by no means failed to reach " The American
Eagle," and when Strong came in Uncle Billy
Green was just expressing himself with regard to
Coakley :

" Of course the Judge'll provide for his man
when he gets a chance. That's where he's sharp.
And if Coakley is smart enough to suit Judge Garvey, he's smart enough to teach *my* children—that's
what *I* say."

A private audience with him would have been
merely postponing the hour of general discussion,
so Strong made a brief exposition of his case—
gently enough, but with considerable force—then
and there, displaying the letter he carried by way
of proof. He hardly expected to elicit anything
but the usual laugh and comment on the Judge's
smartness. But there was a marked seriousness of
tone in the remarks when he ended.

" Well, that *is* pretty rough."

" Yes, sir, that's going too far. The Judge
ought to know where to stop. I don't stand by no

man when it comes to a.shabby trick on an unpro-
tected school-marm."

" A real lady, too—I could see that when she
went by with you, Strong."

Even Green said, uneasily, "No, I shouldn't
think the Judge ought to do that, quite."

It was evident that Green's Ferry drew its lines
as much as any other town. The moral support it
offered Strong was mainly negative, however, and
Green, after several alternate conversations with
his two fellow trustees during this Saturday evening, went off early Sunday morning to visit his
married daughter at the old Meeker place, leaving
word that they must fix it between them. Judge
Garvey closed the somewhat stormy conference of
Saturday evening with a promise to break down
Miss Northrop's school in a week, and Strong's
paper in a month. "Do you flatter yourself I
should not have had your contemptible sheet in
powder under my feet, sir, before this, if I had
thought it worth the attention ?" Nevertheless, as
there was nothing on which the Judge prided himself more than on his invariable civility to ladies
("the courtly Judge" was his favorite phrase in
writing up a local notice of any affair at which he
had been present), Strong, having possession of the
school-house key, was able to put Miss Northrop
into possession on Monday morning without opposition. The Judge even visited her during the day
and addressed the school with extreme suavity.

He was, however, very seriously affronted, and

had not passed his Sunday without diligent preparation among parents and children to make Miss Northrop's position untenable. It would have been no difficult task, either, but for an altogether unprecedented obstacle—a factor that he had not dreamed of in his calculations, and that Strong himself had underestimated. The children, who had gone to school Monday morning primed for mutiny, surrendered their hearts in a body to Miss Northrop by night ; three days later, Uncle Billy Green's niece, who taught the primary school, gave in adoring allegiance ; by the end of the week everybody who had seen her was her advocate. It was certainly an unprecedented thing that Judge Garvey's best exertions should come to naught, because of a woman's way of smiling and speaking ; but Miss Northrop's tenure of the school was secure. It was not entirely speech and smile, however. Miss Northrop was interested in everything, and consequently had common ground with everybody ; and she met each one on that ground, not so much ignoring as temporarily forgetting differences.

The year wore on from gray to gray ; the parching north wind poured down the plain and darkened the air with gritty dust ; the sky, though cloudless, grew murkier every day. Then the wind shifted to the south, and the sky grew darker yet with surging heaps of clouds, and at last down came the late November rain ; and next morning Miss Northrop could see, like a miracu-

lous creation of the night, up and down every east-
and-west street, a range of azure mountains along
either horizon, snow-crowned, clear-cut, against
an exquisite blue sky. Every two or three weeks
the surge of clouds would come rolling up with the
south wind, and the rain would come down in tor-
rents for days, till the Sacramento, yellow with
mud, roared level with its banks ; and then the
storm would break away, and there would be a
week or two of blue sky and brilliant air and green
earth.

One Sunday in March, between the early and
the latter rains, Miss Northrop and Will Strong
walked out together several miles over the plain.
The gravel had long disappeared under green bur-
clover and *filaria*, thickly dotted with the little
yellow clover blossoms, the lilac ones of the *filaria*,
and with small blue gilias. The flocks and herds
had been driven down from the mountains where
they spend their summers and autumns, and the
air was full of the bleating of lambs. Up and
down either horizon, converging toward the north,
were the long ranks of the Sierras and Coast
Range, deep blue, ruggedly tipped with white
peaks of all shapes—the Lassen Buttes, the Yallo
Balleys, and many a lesser one. Northward, in
the interval between the ranges, miles and miles
away, the solitary peak of Shasta rose above the
dark oak-knolls, sharp-white from base to tip,
against a stainless sky. They sat down on the
warm clover, beside a noisy yellow stream that ran

full to its banks on its way to the Sacramento.
Winifred pushed back her hat, dropped her hands
in her lap, and let her senses be played upon by
the delicious air, the blue and white of mountains
and sky and clouds, the luminous green, the rushing of water close by, and the bleating of flocks in
the distance. It gave Will a good chance to watch
her face—the sweetness of the mouth ; the nobility
of the level brows ; the frankness of the eyes ; the
soft wave of her hair. There was a marked sadness in her face in repose ; to wonder why, was to
transgress the code of loyal humility that Will set
himself ; he had not even considered it due chiv-
alry to speculate, much less ask, as to the reason
of so amazing a phenomenon as her presence in
California at all, and the incongruity of her school-
teaching. Her pose was perfect, and yet nothing
could be more unconscious. Was that marvellous
spontaneity, that simple dignity, the regular thing
among the men and women Winifred belonged
with ? It made him feel left very far out to think
so. How incapable of effort for admiration she
was, yet how invariably admirable !

She caught him looking at her, in time. " What
is it ?" she said, simply.

He colored with some confusion, but confessed
a piece of his thought. " I was wondering if you
really do not care at all for admiration. Most
people would think they got the good of their living
in being praised a fraction as much as you've been.
If that's impertinent I beg your pardon ; you
asked me."

The portion of aristocrat's pride that was in Winifred was largely concentrated in an objection to talking of herself or letting other people do it ; so she looked a little annoyed. She began with some constraint :

" Yes—I care—at first—when it is the right one that praises. But there is always a reaction of self-distrust. It seems humiliating," she went on more frankly, " to have been praised for having done some common thing— solved a problem, or written a poem, or handled a piano—a little more or less cleverly, when one comes to think what education and art are. And *personal* admiration— that always seems a contemptible sort of folly, if you think of what great things there are to do and be in the world, and the lives the great lonely souls have lived."

" Your achievement seems little to you," said Will, with some gloom, " because, I suppose, more always opens to you. To me, who have made none—"

" Why, Will," she cried, with the most genuine dissent. " You have done more than almost any one I know. Do you call it nothing to do a college curriculum alone and under all sorts of hindrances ? And I know that it was done well and thoroughly."

" Oh, yes," he said, indifferently, tossing bits of clover into the stream, " I could have passed an A. B. fast enough. But you know better than I do, Winifred, that that's the least of a college course. I've seen fellows that had to work their way through and had no spare time or energy, and they always lacked a great deal of the college flavor ; the education didn't permeate 'em. Then there are other things—music, art, social opportunities, capacity of expression—that are no slight things to miss ; they make up more of first-class living than Greek optatives or the equation of a surface. It isn't really possible for a man, not backed by circumstances, to get himself into a position that some are born to." He let the clover be and looked up. " Oh, I'm not growling, Winifred," he said, hastily, smiling, as he saw her about to speak eagerly. " I'm only making philosophical observations, and using myself as an illustration. Why in the world should I growl to find myself stranded half way up, when there is a townful of people behind us clear down at the bottom, and no more their fault than mine ? Why should I mind that I am left out from the best chances, any more than that a thousand other fellows are ? ' What Act of Legislature was there that ' *I* should be cultured ?"

She was leaning forward with her irresistible eyes full on his, and face and voice vivified with that sympathetic expressiveness that makes speech count for far more than the words.

" Will, that is true," she cried, " but it is only part of the truth. ' Close thy ' Carlyle ; ' open thy ' Emerson. It's true, you have missed some things that you deserved to have and that many of your inferiors have for nothing. But your life is only

begun, and your ability and pluck can do so much
that you needn't waste regret on anything they
may fail to do. Even if circumstances be uncon-
querable that stand between you and some good
things, are the things you have gained instead of
less value ?—your courage and patience, your
self-reliance and trustworthiness and helpfulness ?
Why, Will, *character* is worth more than knowledge of art, or familiarity with good society ; just
to live bravely is worth more than all the rest.
Do you suppose I would exchange your com-
panionship for that of a dozen ' cultured ' people
who could talk to me about ' sincere furniture ' "
—this was in the last decade, remember—" and
Rauss's heads, as you can't, and who never showed
me one spark of genuine feeling about the great
things of life, as you can ?"

Will was overwhelmed. Winifred had talked of
his affairs much, following them with unvarying
interest, but of himself or herself, never ; and it
was actually a new idea to the young fellow that
she could have any very high opinion of him.
Moreover, it was the first time he had heard her
speak with unveiled and ardent feeling.   ·

" You do not mean"—and he formed his words
with difficulty—" that I could meet on equal
ground people that—such people as *your* associ-
ates."

" No ; you would meet most of them on higher
ground. If they didn't know it, that would be
their discredit. I should think you could see

ʹ

that," she added, in a quick, parenthetic averse way, "from *their* associate. If you want to get a higher opinion of the value of your life, compare it with an ordinary, foolish, useless one—like mine." She gave him no chance to answer that, but was the next moment on her feet, suggesting that they walk on, and wishing they were not to stop short of the Lassen Buttes, whose apparent nearness, scores of miles distant as they were, was still a perpetual surprise to her eastern eyes.

When everything has been made ready for it, a few sentences may easily make or mark an era in life ; and it is probable that if Miss Northrop had not in effect told young Strong he was quite good enough for her, he might have remained her contented vassal for years. Six months of being her nearest friend worked their result, to be sure ; but the humility they were gnawing at was of mediævally tough fibre, and of twice six years' growth. His depreciation of himself, however, had only meant sense of distance from her ; therefore, his sense of the significance of her speech was enormous. He felt his relation to her changed ; he was shaken from all his moorings, and thrown into a mighty agitation that possessed him night and day, and only grew with time. For this was what it all came to : Was the distance between Winifred and himself greater than the distance between her and any other man ? And when he had once thought that, the gate was open, and the besieging host marched in and took possession of every corner of him with longing and desire and a madness of tenderness.

He thought of nothing else. He wrote his editorials and set type under an unceasing sense of it, as people have done brain-work and finger-work to an accompaniment of unceasing physical pain. For there was nothing joyous about it to him ; it was all a bitter pain of mad desire to be something to her—to secure her, somehow, before this great, dark future swept her away from him. And yet the latter rains came and went, the green faded from the ground, the mountains grew dimmer and duller, and at last disappeared in the summer murk, before he took in his own mind the next step—from lover to suitor, as before from vassal to lover.

He did so simply because he could not stand it any longer. It stood to reason that there must be a way out of such active torments. And, after all, why not he as well as any other man ? It was absurd to suppose that Winifred could ever be *in love* with any man, as a man would be with her. It occurred to Will that the thing to do was natural enough, after all—not to ask Winifred's love, but to offer her his. And he walked down to Mrs. Stutt's to do it, one August evening, a little before school opened after vacation. He was in good spirits, too ; to come to action and to speech, after so long repression, was an inestimable relief. And she had been doubly friendly to him all this time.

Mrs. Stutt was in her little strip of grass and oleanders. "That you, Mr. Strong?" she called out cheerily as he lifted the gate-latch. "Well, Miss Northrop's in the sitting-room, I s'pose. You go right in, and I'll come in when I've done my watering."

"Thank you," said Will, absently, and walked on into the house. Winifred was not in the dark little sitting-room. He walked to the open window and stood there, expecting her to come in presently. There were veils of Madeira vine over the window, just opening their whitish tassels of bloom, and the air was full of the smell of them. Mrs. Stutt began to water the grass outside, and the shower of water from her hose glimmered through the Madeira vine ; the noise of the water came to him, and the crying of crickets, and the smell of the freshly wet earth. Then he heard a step on the porch, and saw Winifred go down the short path to the gate. He could see by her white dress that she stood still there ; so he went out, too, to join her. Mrs. Stutt was watering at the other side of the house now, and the two were alone.

Will stopped a moment in the darkness and faint odor of a great oleander, a few feet from the motionless girl at the gate, to realize well the grace of her dim white figure, and her unconscious attitude. She stood in a weary way, with her head a little fallen back, and her hands hanging loosely clasped before her. There was so much and so incomprehensible emotion in the attitude, that

Will felt vaguely thrust out into another world from that where her interests lay. She had not heard him approach, for the train from the south was just coming to a stand at the station, not a stone's throw off, and there was a great noise of jarring cars, and shouting men, and escaping steam, and ringing bell. He waited till the noise should be quite over. Some one came walking rapidly from the station ; Will, glancing at the dark figure, thought it had, even in this dimness, an unfamiliar look. It paused close by the gate.

" Winifred !"

Will did not know the voice ; the tone turned him blind and dizzy.

Winifred started violently, and turned ; she clasped her hands tightly, and lifted them to her breast in a frightened way, as she fell back a step.

" Oh, my God !" she cried, under her breath. There was a rattle of the gate-latch, a sharp flying open of the gate, and the stranger held her in his arms.

" My darling, my darling !" he said, with an infinite tenderness. " Did you think you could hide anywhere in all this wide world where I should not find you ?"

For just an instant she yielded to his clasp—then she drew back. " You must not," she said, softly, with unmistakable pain in her voice. " You know. that. I thought if I was utterly out of sight or hearing, you would forget me, and *I* might—forget myself."

He broke in before she had fairly spoken. " You were mistaken, Winifred ; there was no one between us. O my foolish little hot-head ! if you had not been so headlong in your self-sacrifice—if you had only waited till I came back—I could have showed you in ten minutes that there was no place for it. Mollie is married to John Gates and is very happy. And you and I—my little girl, how nearly our two lives have been spoiled ! Sweetheart," he said, laughing with a shaky voice, " I think I shall never dare let go of you again"—and he drew her back to him.

She hesitated—surrendered—clung to him with a long sobbing breath. " Oh, I have wanted you so, I have *wanted* you so !" she cried. " Oh, don't be a dream and melt away this time !"

Will Strong, standing close in the darkness of the oleander, acquiring a life-long association with smell of Madeira vine and oleander and wet earth, cry of crickets and noise of sprinkling water, gathered himself together enough to creep away. He was *going* to realize it pretty soon, he thought ; he did not yet ; it seemed likely to be beyond endurance when he did. As he passed the door some one opened it, and the lamp-light streamed about him ; Winifred looked around and saw his face for an instant, and then he had slipped away through a side gate.

He walked out from town across miles of dark plain, until he came to the empty channel of the stream by which they had sat in March. Under-

foot not a blade of grass or green thing; no
stranger would have believed that living thing had
ever grown there. The flocks and herds had long
since gone to the mountain pastures. The dry
channel between shelvy banks of gravel showed
white in the unclouded yet dull starlight. The air
was lifeless, and faintly tainted with smoke from
forest fires in the mountains.

Will threw himself down on his face, clutching
with his fingers at the gritty dirt. He knew as
surely then, looking forward to his life, as he will
know at the end looking back, that this would
never be an out-lived romance. Nor could he
creep back into that temple of dreams from which
Winifred's own hand had lured him—it had crum-
bled to dust behind him. Nor was he like one
who, losing a woman, loses only his best pleasure
and best ambition ; she was the vital condition to
every pleasure, every ambition ; losing her, he lost
all. The realization clutched him by this time
like a tiger. There was not a living creature
within miles ; a man might go down to primal
depths, might drop even the restraint of the human
in outcries and struggles as free as a tortured
beast's. It may be that solitude sees more such
scenes than a decently decorous world would like
to think.

Yet there was a sense upon him of some moral
demand, some decision to be made ; and in time
he began to try to collect himself for it. It would
seem as if there could hardly be a position that

left less for him to decide. There was no question
of renouncing—he had never had anything to
renounce. Nevertheless, his instinct was correct
in urging him to a moral conflict and a momentous
decision. The question was simply whether he
could pick up his life again, could find faith that
anything was worth living for ; or whether life
was to be a hollow going through the forms—frus-
trated, purposeless, full of brooding regret and
jealousy, shame, and sense of wrong. But he
could not drag his bruised mind up to the question ; he could not even think what it was. He
lifted himself up, stepped down into the dry
channel, and knelt on the white stones, obeying
old association with the attitude ; laid his arms
and head on a shelf of the bank, and let the
stunned and nerveless will lie passive, while the
accumulated forces of years—of generations—passion and pain and despair and love, shame and
bitterness and loyalty—trampled back and forth
over him, fighting out for him his battle.

It was deathly, aggressively still ; not an insect
to chirp, not a tree to rustle ; only bare earth and
sodden air. After a long time Will raised his head
and threw it back, looking up at the dull stars,
while his outstretched hands lay clasped before
him ; he began to breathe more deeply. Not
many minutes later he rose and walked homeward
across the dim, wide waste.

It was afternoon of the next day when he stood
at Mrs. Stutt's door again. Mrs. Stutt looked at

him with the embarrassment of conscious pity as
she admitted him. People had been looking at
him all day, on the street and in the office, with
the same embarrassment and pity. Miss Northrop
was packing, the good woman said ; and, in an
answer to her call, Winifred came out from her
room into the little sitting-room. She, too, was
evidently under agitation and embarrassment.
Will had no doubt, from his first sight of her face,
that she had seen and understood his haggard
flight the evening before. He was himself entirely
calm, as he held out his hand with a grave smile
in silence.

Winifred tried to speak naturally.

" I had just sent a note to you, Will,'' she said,
as they sat down.

"About the school, I suppose," he answered,
quietly. " You are going away at once ?"

"Yes." There she stopped, with her eyes
downcast. She looked up to his face and caught
her breath to speak, stopped, and began again.

" You have been very good to me all this year—''
there she hesitated. Her difficulty was to choose
her words so as to ignore his secret, and yet not
part from him in a cold or inadequate way.

He rose, and crossed over to her.

" Winifred," he said gently, " you are distressed
on my account ; and so it is better that I should
speak of what otherwise it would be better to
ignore. I want you to know that you have not
harmed me.''

She rose quickly at that, and they stood near together, with their eyes fixed on each other's ; the fulness of expression in her face seemed to take the place of answer. He went on steadily, speaking low :

" I have thought it all over, and I find these two things stronger than any pain that may have come to me. Winifred, I cannot do you this wrong, to make you the instrument of evil to me. That is one of the two things. And the other is that there is nothing to reproach any one with ; no one has done wrong ; there is no cause for shame, or resentment, or bitterness—only for clean pain. Pain is no great evil, Winifred, when it is clean, no matter how sharp."

He smiled at her tranquilly enough as he spoke. In truth, he was not unhappy at the moment. It is not during but after the parting interview that the pinch comes. She answered him only with her deeply attentive look, and he went on :

" I did not come to those convictions ; they came to me ; or rather, they were in me, and bore down all the other feelings. All the noisy passions dropped away before them, and left just those clear voices in my soul. They made all my love and loyalty work together, instead of tearing me in opposite directions. For, see, Winifred, hasn't it been our moral faith for years that to do spiritual harm to another is the greatest evil that can befall one, and to do him spiritual benefit, the greatest good ? All these years since we were in school

together, I have been proud to think that it could
be only a good to you to have me think of you as
I have thought, because it was only a good to me.
And I will not be so disloyal now as to let my life
be spoiled because of you."

Winifred looked at him aghast. "All these
years!" It was a revelation intolerable at first
shock to a woman that was no coquette.

"I think it was all the time dimly in my mind
what *your* last year had been ; at last I went out of
my life and into yours. I want you to understand
that I do not think of it with bitterness, because I
entered so little into it ; I realize, Winifred "—his
voice broke from its steadiness—"that you have
been good, *good* in it all. If you had not been—if
you had trifled with me—I think I should be at the
bottom of the river to-day. But since no one has
wronged me," he went on more quietly, "since
nothing monstrous or unnatural has befallen me,
everything I believed in has the same claim on me
as ever.

"And I want you to know that you need not
mind my love, Winifred." She dropped her eyes
and stood mute. "It is something you may be
willing and glad to have without troubling yourself because you cannot return it. For any pain
that has happened, do not trouble yourself about
that either—if I don't mind it, you needn't," he
said, smiling a little, with a certain manly sweetness quite new to him. "I find one gains some-

thing in having no longer to struggle with pain and try to keep her at arm's length."

She looked up then, and cried out passionately. "O Will, Will, if only there was anything in all this world I could do to make it up to you !"

"There is nothing to make up," he said. "I would rather have pain from you than pleasure from any one else. But there *is* something that you can do ; this : not to feel my love a burden laid upon you, an annoyance or trespass, an anxiety or self-reproach—or anything that will make you want to get rid of it," he finished, smiling again ; "and to let me give you all I wish, on the condition that I ask no return. And if, in a few years, I should ask to come and live near you, and be good friends—may I ? It would be hard," he urged, less quietly, "that I should have to lose your friendship, when I ask nothing more. Would you take away the crumbs from me, just because I have lost the loaf ?"

"Is that best, Will ?" she began, anxious and hesitating. "Oh, I mean for you. It isn't *possible* that you can always—think of me—so. There is no reason. If you do not see me—somebody else—"

"Have I been seeing you these dozen years ?" he said, very gently. "You may trust me to know what is best for me. Why think—think a moment, dear friend, and you will understand. You, of all people, *can* understand the plane I want you to take me on."

Winifred's eyes kindled and her face flushed.
" I see. I *do* understand. I can meet you on your
own plane, and I can trust your friendship and
you. I am not afraid to have you come—after a
year or two."

" Thank you," he said, shaken as he had not
been.

" It is because you are very noble that any good
can come out of this harm," she went on, with an
eloquent tremor in her voice. " I can see that
before very long I shall be, as you said, willing—
glad—for so great a gift—only always sorry for
your sake. I am very grateful *now*—I cannot tell
you how great a thing I think it is—from such a
man as you."

They had both become embarrassed and shy
now, and both stood silent to recover their ease.
" You leave by this evening's train ?" he asked in
a minute.

" Yes."

" Then this is good-by."

" For a while."

They moved together to the door. As they
reached it, Will turned and held out his hand, with
an attempt at a smile. They stood a few moments
with hands clasped. Winifred's downcast eyes
were filling.

" Good-by, Winifred," he said.

" Good-by," she answered, faintly. A minute
later she had thrown herself sobbing on her bed,
and he was walking down the street.

He met Winifred's lover, coming from the ticket-office—a gentleman high-bred and handsome in every line, a scholar by his appearance, a good man by his eyes, a good companion by his smile. There were all those differences between him and Will that the young man had talked of and Winifred in all sincerity had called nothing ; and, moreover, she would never in the world have loved him if there had not been. The girl was an aristocrat after all, when it came to a question not of friendship but love. And Will knew it ; love is penetrating enough to divine that much from scanty data. He looked at the stranger with a sort of transferred reverence—what a king of men must he be whom Winifred could crown ! And if he did not look at him without a blinding pang, it was, nevertheless, a test of the thoroughness of the night's work that there was neither bitterness nor aversion in it. Something, that sense of having disarmed pain—not dodged nor outwitted it, but disarmed it forever—must have been in Winkelried's consciousness as the spears pressed in.

But, after all, it is *taking* the second place that costs—not being there after it has been once sincerely and thoroughly accepted. Bunyan knew long ago that it was easy walking in the Valley of Humiliation, once you had come safely down.

On the street an acquaintance met Strong and turned to walk beside him. It was the man who would not trust Judge Garvey out of sight with his baby's silver mug.

"I was just going to your office," he said. "It's something very important." He spoke with a marked friendliness, and a transparently covert sympathy. "You see," he went on, confidentially, "we fellows that have been against Garvey begin to think our minority's about over. The whole affair of Miss Northrop has hurt him. He was shabby when first she came, about that Coakley business, and he's been ugly about her ever since in a sneaking sort of way. Such a lady, too! And there's a thing come out to-day—if you'll excuse my speaking of it." He showed a certain embarrassment. "Uncle Billy Green gave it away first—he knew, being postmaster— but Garvey's been boasting of it himself, too, in the bar-room. You know you used to write to a fellow in the States, and haven't written to him so much lately."

"Yes, I know," said Strong. The man caught a hint of what he did not say in what he did.

"Uncle Billy gives away any interesting point he gets in the post-office," he said, apologetically. "You knew that before, Strong. Well, Garvey got out of him, too, that Miss Northrop didn't have nor write any letters; and he got it into his head she was hiding. Anybody could see she wasn't used to working for a living—"

"Look here—"

"Bless you, Strong, I sha'n't say a word disrespectful to her. This is something you'd ought to know. He just did up a 'Clarion' with some

notice about the school in it, and her name
marked, and sent it to that fellow you used to
write to ; and he wrote on the margin : ' Please
forward to Miss N.'s friends.'   He said in the bar-
room, to-day, that he didn't know just what would
come of it, but it stood to reason if she was on the
hide, it would damage her or you, somehow."

"It hasn't, however," said Strong.   "But if *I*
stayed round the bar-room—"

"Oh, we choked him off.   I tell you, Strong,
everybody thinks it was a pretty dirty trick.   The
people don't care so much about his big tricks, but
they won't stand any such small ones.   No money
in it, either—only spite !   Well, the long and the
short is—it's only a few weeks till convention ; and
if you'll take hold now while they're mad, you can
name your own man for Senate, and we'll send
you to Assembly."

"I don't want to go to Assembly," said Will,
standing on his office-step.   "I'll gladly do my
best to defeat Garvey for Senate."

"Well, you just decide on your man, and bring
him out in your next paper and we'll elect him.
The people are strong for you just now.   And I
should think you would look on going to Assembly as a sort of duty—purify politics, you know."

"Well—I'll think about it."   And young Strong
walked into his shabby office, stopped to give Jim
directions, then went in behind his screen, and
sat down to write a proper editorial for beginning
the reform campaign.

HOW OLD WIGGINS WORE SHIP.

AN OLD SAILOR'S YARN.

By Captain Roland T. Coffin.

"WELL, sir," said the old sailor, "here we are ag'in. I ain't been round here much lately, and atwixt you and me, she's put the 'kybosh' onto it, holdin' that comin' round here and hystin' are promotin' of rheumatics, which, as are well known, they come of long and various exposures in all climates, to say nothin' of watchin' onto a damp dock night arter night continual. But what's the use? Everybody knows as a quiet home are better than silver and fine gold, which it stands to reason are to be obtained in two ways. Wimmin are like sailors in some respects ; whoever has anythin' to do with 'em must either be saddled and bridled, leastwise, or else booted and spurred. You've got to ride 'em, or else they'll ride

.*. *The World*, N. Y., *November*, 1873.

you. Bein' a sailorman myself, it ain't likely as
I'd say anythin' ag'in 'em ; but if the truth must
be told, I'll say this—that while it'll never do, not
at no price, for to let sailors git the upper hand,
there's many a man as has giv' the helm into the
hands of his old woman and made a better v'yage
thereby ; and I don't mind sayin', sir, that havin'
while follerin' the water got into the habit of al-
lowin' her for to be skipper in the house durin' my
short stoppin's on shore, it got for to be so much
the custom, that since comin' home for a full due I
ain't never tried for to break away from it ; and
though human natur' is falliable, and she does make
mistakes, especially about the hystin', on the
whole, and by and large, I judges I've been a
gainer by it, as I believes at least eight men out of
ten would be if they took the hint accordin' and
went and done likewise.

"I don't go for to say as she ever goes to go
to say I ain't a-goin' for to let you go there ; but
it are terrible aggrivokin' when the rheumatics
twinges awful, and as it might be that this saw-
mill don't want no more splinters laid onto it,
to have her feelin'ly remark, ' Well, if you will
go round a-guzzlin' ale with your swell friends
and a-leavin' your lawful wife to home alone
you must expect to pay for it,' whereas I know
it are the dock and other causes long gone by ;
but that knowledge don't ease the pain a mor-
sel, and the last time I were that way tantalized
I swore I wouldn't come here no more.   But what-

ever are the use ? Man resolves and reresolves and
then takes another snifter, and so here I are, and
bein' as its cold, as so she sha'n't have no basis for
her unfeelin' remark about guzzlin' ale, we'll let
him make it hot rum, and arter the old receipt,
neither economizin' in the rum or the sugar, but
givin' a fair drink for honest money.

"Well, well (just mix another afore the glass
cools off), to think how the time goes. Here it are
autumn ag'in, and in a few weeks 'twill be winter.
It reminds me (I'll take one more, if you please,
with one lump less of sugar and the space in rum)
that I'm gittin' old, and I feels it. My eyes ain't
so good and my legs ain't so good, and I ain't so
good all over. When I goes down to the dock my
lantern are heavier than it used to were, and the
distance ain't so short as it used to seem from the
dock to the house. Afore many years I'll be put
quietly away, and though I'd prefer bein' beauti-
fully sewed up and launched shipshape in blue
water, with a hundred pound weight for to keep
me down, I s'poses it won't make much difference,
nohow. Anyhow, if I lives as long as old Wiggins,
I hopes I may go as well at the eend. I don't
think I ever told you about him, and if you'll let
him fill 'em up ag'in—for it's one of the vartues
of hot rum that the more you drinks the thirstier
you gits—I'll reel you the yarn right off.

"Old Wiggins had been all his life into the
Liverpool trade and had got well fixed, so far as
cash were consarned ; and so when he came for to

be seventy or seventy-two years old he were persuaded for to knock off for a full due and spend the
balance of his life ashore.   Goin' up to some place
in Connecticut, he buys hisself a place there and
settles down.   Well, for a time he were all right,
a-fixin' up his house, a-buildin' new barns and
hen-coops and fences and the like, and I've heerd
tell that the house where he kep' his pigs were
better than any dwellin'-house in that region, and
the whole place were the wonder of the country
roundabout ; but arter he had fixed his house all
up like a ship, with little staterooms all through
the upper part of it, and had got everythin' inside
and out in shipshape order, and there weren't
nothin' else he could think of for to do, he gits
terribly homesick and discontented, and times
when he'd come to the city for to collect his sheer
of the profits of ships as he had a interest in, he'd
sit for hours on the wharf a-watchin' the vessels
on the river, and it were like drawin' teeth for to
git him to leave and go up to his home.   His eyes
had giv' out sometime afore he quit the sea, and
his legs was shaky, so as he had to walk with a
settin' pole, and his hand were tremblin' and un-
steady ; but aloft he were still all right, and his
head were as clear as a bell.

   "Arter bein' ashore a matter of seven year, he
comes to town one day to see a ship off what he
had been in afore he quit, and in which he had a
half interest.   The skipper of that ship, which her
name were the Vesuvius, he bein' called Perkins,

in comin' from the Custom House arter clearin', got athwart-hawse of a dray and were knocked down, the wheels passin' over his legs and breakin' of 'em, and whatever do old Wiggins do—the home-sickness bein' strong onto him—but says to the agents, ' It are a pity for to lose a day's fair wind ; I'll go aboard and take her out myself ; ' and, sure enough, he done it, never lettin' on to the folks at home, but leavin' the agents to tell 'em arter he were gone.

" Into that ship I were shipped, she bein' 830 tons or thereabout, with three royal yards across, and loaded with flour and grain, there bein' sixteen of us afore the mast, with two mates, carpenter and cook, and steward, leavin' on the 16th of November, and, unless I'm mistakened, in the year 1843.

" We towed down to the Hook and out over the bar, and then put the muslin on to her with a fine breeze from sou'west, and I supposes there weren't a happier man in the world than old Wiggins when he discharged the pilot and steamer and took charge.

" ' I've giv' 'em the slip,' says he to the mate. ' I've giv' 'em the slip ; they thought I were too old for to go to sea, but I'll show 'em thar's plenty of life into me yet ; git out all the starboard stunsails and see to it that she's kep' a-movin' night and day, for in sixteen days I expects to walk the pierhead in Liverpool.' Well, sure enough, a-movin' she were kep', and I never seen harder

carryin's on than I seen that passage ; but we
never lost a stitch of canvas, 'cause the old man
not only knowed how to carry it, but he knowed
how to take it off of her when it be to come off,
and in a gale of wind he'd •liven up wonderful,
whereas in light weather he'd show his age.   It
were funny for to see him takin' the sun and
tryin' to read her off, which he weren't able for to
do, not by no means.

"' What d'ye stand on ? ' he'd say to the mate
arter screwin' his eye to the glass and tryin' to
make it out ; and when the mate would tell him,
he'd say, ' I believe that agrees with me ; just take
a squint at my instrument ; my eyesight ain't just
as good as it used for to be, and I don't quite
make it out.'   Then the mate would read him off
his instrument, and arter he'd made it eight bells
he'd go down and work it up and prick her off.
The fourteenth day out we made the light on Fast-
net Rock, off Cape Clear, and went bowlin' along
the coast, passin' Tuskar next day, and swingin'
her off up channel and round Hollyhead past the
Skerries and takin' a pilot off P'int Lynas.   It
were a sight worth seein' for to watch the old man
handle her in takin' a pilot.   The wind were fresh
from west-norwest, and we passed the Skerries with
all three royals set and lower topmast and to'gallan'
stunsails on the port side.   As soon as ever we
passed the rocks we kep' off for Lynas, and as soon
as the stunsails got by the lee they was hauled in.
Then with the wind about two p'ints on the star-

board quarter we went bilin' along for the boat
which we seen standin' off shore just to the east'ard
of the P'int. There were a pretty bubble of a sea
on, and afore we gits to him he goes about standin'
in to the bay and givin' sheet. We follers along
arter him, goin' two feet to his one, still carryin' all three royals, with hands at halliards
and clewlines. Just afore we gits to him the old
man sings out, ' Clew up the royals, haul down
the flyin' jib, haul up the crochick and mainsail.'
By this time we was well under the land and in
smooth water. Keepin' his eye onto the pilot-
boat, which were a couple of p'ints onto our
weather bow, the old man no sooner seen her come
to than he sings out, ' Hard up the helm ! ' And
as we swung off afore the wind we runned up the
foresail and laid the head-yards square ; then
mannin' the port main braces we let the to'gallan'
yards run down on the caps and let her come to
ag'in, and so nicely had the old man calculated the
distance that as she come to the wind she shot up
alongside of the pilot-boat, stoppin' just abreast of
her and not over twenty foot away.

" ' That was well done, Mr. Mate,' said the pilot,
as he come over the side ; ' some of these galoots
makes us chase 'em half a day afore we can board
'em. Fill away the head-yards, put your helm up,
run up the flyin' jib, brail up the spanker check in
the arter yards,' and as she swung off he comes aft
to the wheel where I was a-steerin', and says, ' Keep
her east-sou'east, my man ; giv' us a chew of ter-

backer.' We soon had the muslin piled onto her
ag'in, and sure enough, as old Wiggins had said,
the sixteenth day out he walked the pierhead in
Liverpool.

"I understood as old Wiggins was made a good
deal on in Liverpool as bein' the oldest skipper
that had ever come there, and the Board of Trade
and what not giv' him dinners, and so on—which,
considerin' his age, he oughtn't to have took—and
by other skippers at the hotel he were much
honored, bein' giv' the head of the table and
treated with great deference—and all this dinin' and
winin' and feastin' weren't no good to him—and,
arter a stay of three weeks, when we ag'in went
down the river with full complement of passengers
and a good freight, he weren't not by no means as
well as when we went in. We had, too, a tough
time down channel, a stiff sou'wester, with rain
and thick weather, and it told onto the old man,
so that when arter bein' out a week we at last got
clear of Tuskar and had the ocean open, the relief
from the strain fetched him, and he were took
down sick.

"Whether it were to punish him for comin' to
sea at his time of life or not I don't know; but
from this on we did have the devil's own weather.
Gale after gale from the west'ard, shiftin' constant
from sou'west to nor'west, and tryin' constant to
see from which quarter it could blow the hardest.

"The mate were a plucky and a able young
feller, by the name of Graham, and he kep' her a-

dancin' as well as the old man would have done.
Constant she had everythin' put to her that she'd
bear, and always were she kep' on the tack where
she'd make the most westin', and so she struggled
along till we was as far as thirty degrees west, we
bein' thirty days out and not yet half way. Every
day we asked the steward how old Wiggins were
a-gittin' on, and every day he'd shake his head
and say 'no better;' and it come to be understood, fore and aft, that it were as much as a toss-
up if the old man ever smelled grass ag'in. We
had a little let-up arter gittin' into the thirties,
and for a day or so had fine weather and a chance
to dry our dunnage. Fine days, however, is scarce
in January on that herrin' pond—I'll take just
another ; mentionin' herrin's makes me dry—and
when you gits 'em they are most always weather-
breeders. I went up on to the main royal yard
when our side come up at 8 o'clock one mornin'
for to sew on the leather on the parral, and it
were like a day in May. Afore I got the leather
sewed on I be to look out for myself, 'cause they
was goin' to clew up the sail, and from that time
on it breezed on from the sou'ard, keepin' us
constantly takin' the sail off of her, till at four
bells we was under double-reefed topsails and
reefed courses, with jib, crochick, and spanker
stowed. We hammered away under this, carryin'
on very heavy, 'cause she were headin' west-
nor'west, which were a good course, till eight bells
in the arternoon watch, when the sea gittin' up so

tremendiously we had to furl the reefed main-sail
and mizzen topsail and close reef the fore and main
topsails.

"You'd think that were snug enough for any
ship, now, wouldn't you? and sartin it are; no
ship ever ought to have less canvas than this, till
it blows away, 'cause she's safer with it onto her
than with it off, the reefed foresail supportin' the
yard. Well, we'd had gales and gales, but this
here gale beat anythin' that I'd ever seen, and at
seven bells in the first night watch, with a tremendious surge, the weather leech rope of the foresail giv' way, and in a jiffy away went the foreyard
in the slings—the foresail and fore-topsail goin'
into ribbons. All hands, of course, was busy
for'ard, tryin' for to git some of this wreck stuff
tranquillized, when all of a suddint from the poop
come the old man's voice, full and round and
clear, and not shrill and pipin' as we'd heerd it
last, and above all the roarin' of the gale and the
din of the slattin' canvas, we heerd him shout:
' Stations for wearin' ship. We must git her head
round to the sou'ard,' he bawled in the ear of the
mate, as Mr. Graham struggled aft; ' the shift will
come in less than half a hour, and its goin' to be
tremendious; if it catches us aback it won't leave
a stick into her; but it ain't a-goin' to catch us,
sir; I've brung her through many and many a time
like this. I'll bring her through this one, and then
you must do the rest. Now, then,' says he, ' stand
by, put your helm just a few spokes a-weather,

don't check her at all with the rudder, slack a foot
or two of the lee braces and check in to wind'ard ;
keep your eye constant on that sail, Mr. Clark '—
that were the second mate—' and don't let it shake ;
keep it good full and give her away; lay the crochick
yard square, and come up to the main-braces, all of
you.' And so, gently, as if she'd been a sick child,
he coaxed her to go off, and she begin to gather
way. As soon as she done so the helm were put
hard up, and the main-yard rounded in, just
keepin' the topsail alift, but not permittin' it to
shake. As she went off till she got the sea on the
quarter, a mighty wave came a-roilin' along, board-
in' us about the main riggin', floodin' the decks
and dashin' out the starboard bulwarks. The minnit we got the wind onto the starboard quarter we
braced the mainyard sharp up with the port-braces
and bowsed the weather ones as taut as a harp
string. 'Now, then,' says the old man, 'never
mind that trash for'ard, let that go ; git a jumper
on to the main-yard and a preventer main-topsail
brace aloft ; lay aloft for your lives, and clap preventer gaskets on everythin' that's furled ; we'll
have it soon from the north'ard fit to take the
masts out of her.' He were right. In a short time
there were a instant's lull, and then with a roar
that were almost deafenin' came the cyclone from
the north. Thanks to the old man's sagacity and
experience, howsever, we was a-headin' sou'-
southeast when it hit us, and it struck us right aft.
   " ' Steady as you go,' shouts the old man, and

then, a minnit arter, as she gathered way, he says
ag'in to the mate, ' We must let her come to, Mr.
Graham, we can't run her in the teeth of the old
s'utherly sea ; ease down the helm and let her
smell of it.'   It was a powerful whiff she took, for
as she come to and felt the force of the wind, all
three to'gallan' masts went short off at the cap, the
main-topsail sheets parted, and 'in an instant there
wasn't a piece of the sail left big enough for a
lady's handkerchief.

" ' That's all it can do,' said the old man to the
mate, bitterly ; ' git this trash on deck as soon as
possible, and git her a-waggin' once more ; I've
brung her through it safe, and am goin' home,'
and with that he dropped onto the poop as dead
as mutton.   He had come on deck bare-headed
and with nothin' on but his drawers and shirt, just
as he had laid in his bunk for a fortnight, and the
exposure had carried him off.   However, he knowed
that the shift were so near nobody ever could tell.
There were no doubt, however, but that his gittin'
her weared round were our salvation.   If that
gust had a-struck us aback our masts would have
gone sartin, and it's a toss-up but what we'd a-
gone down starn fust afore she'd a-backed round.
Next day we giv' old Wiggins a funeral fit for the
Emperor of Rooshy, and he well desarved it.   I
don't know as ever I seen a prettier sew-up than we
done on him, wrappin' him first in the American
ensign and then kiverin' him with brand-new No 4
canvas.   Considerin' the sails we'd lost and how

much we needed the canvas, I think he must have been satisfied that we done the handsome thing by him. The day was beautiful and clear, although the wind still blowed a gale. We hadn't been able to do much with the wreck stuff, except git lashin's onto it for to keep it from swingin' about, and we hadn't dared for to try for to send up another maintopsail. We had set the reefed mainsail for to steady her, and that were all. The three to'gallan' masts was still a-hangin' over the side, and the ribbons of the foresail and fore topsail was still a-flutterin' in the breeze, when at eight bells, at midday, all hands was called for to bury the dead. Everythin' that we had in the way of nice clothes we had put on for to do honor to our captain, and most of us was able to sport white shirts and broadcloth. We laid the old man onto a plank and kivered him with the union jack, and all hands gathered round him, while Mr. Graham read the sarvice. Everythin' went lovely, and just at the proper time we tilted the plank, and he slipped off without a hitch of any kind. Arter the mate finished the readin', he said, ' Men, there's a good man gone arter a long life of great usefulness. He were a sailor and a gentleman. I don't think as we ought for to cry over sich a man, and I propose we giv' him three cheers and God bless him ' ; and heartier cheers was never giv' than we giv' that day, arter which all hands got dinner.''

"—— MAS HAS COME."

BY LEONARD KIP.

IT was called Beacon Ledge fully fifty years before the present lighthouse had been built
upon it. For it was' said that long ago, when
wrecking was a profitable trade along the coast,
and goodly vessels were frequently, by false lights,
decoyed to their destruction, there was no more favorable point for the exercise of that systematic
villainy than this rocky, high-lifted bluff. Projecting three or four hundred feet into the sea, with a
gradually curved, sweeping line, it formed, to be
sure, upon the one side, a limited anchorage—safe
enough for those who knew it; but, upon the other
side, it looked upon a waste of shoal, dotted, here
and there, at lowest tide, with craggy breakers, and,
at high water, smooth, smiling, and deceitful, with
the covered dangers. Here, then, upon certain dark
and stormy nights, the flaming beacon of destruc-

.*. *Overland Monthly, January,* 1870.

tion would glow brightly against the black sky, and wildly lighten up the cruel faces of those who stood by and piled on the fagots, while gazing eagerly out to sea to mark the effect of their evil machinations. Nor was it until some thirty years ago that the gangs of wretches were thoroughly broken up, and this, their favorite vantage-ground, wrested from them, and the tall, white lighthouse there securely founded—maintaining in mercy what had before been held as a blighting curse; lifting itself, like a nation's warning finger, and with its calm, serene glow, pointing out the path of safety. Then, in the mouths of all the surrounding inhabitants, Beacon Ledge became known as Beacon Ledge Beacon, and so kept its name, in spite of tautological criticism, or of different and more formal christening, by Government authority.

Still, there hung around the place the memories or traditions of past violence, shipwreck, and murder—partly true, perhaps, but, doubtless, generally false, having only a few grains of fact or probability mingled with all kinds of distorted fictions— the deeds of pirates being supplemented to those of mere wreckers; the imaginations of fishermen along the coast ever inventing plenteous horrors, and wild tales of buccaneering rovers, originally written for other localities, being now wilfully adopted and here located, until, at last, there was hardly a known crime which could not find its origin or counterpart at Beacon Ledge, and the whole neighboring shore became a melancholy storehouse of

terrors, disaster, and distress. These tales being
discovered to be very pleasing to most strangers,
were carefully cultivated and enlarged upon by
each interested denizen of the place ; and to me,
also, for awhile, they had a peculiar charm. I sel-
dom grew tired of hearing some grizzled, tar-in-
crusted fisherman reel off his tissue of improbable
abominations. For awhile, I say, since there came,
at last, a day when I cared no longer for such
bloody traditions, forgot the shadowy horrors that
flitted about the spot, and only thought and cared
for it as the place where I had met and loved dear
little Jessie Barkstead.

She was the only child of the lighthouse keeper.
In a worldly point of view, therefore, was it wisely
done that I should have set my affections upon her?
Possibly not ; and it is likely that, had I known the
weakness of my mind, I would have shunned the danger from the very first. But I was gay and reckless
in my poor self-complacency and deceitful as-
surance of inner strength ; and long before I had
fairly realized how rapidly I was drifting, I
found myself whirling down the swift current,
and was lost. Nor was it a marvel that this should
have so happened. To one who sits aloof in his
unromantic, distant home, it is an easy thing, indeed, to moralize about matters of inferior station
and *mésalliance ;* but I believe that few could have
seen little Jessie, as she first appeared to me, and
not have felt some secret inclination to give way
before those subtile charms of beauty and man-

ner which invested her. Moreover, let it here be mentioned that she was not at all of humble birth or education. Old Barkstead was himself a gentleman by culture and station, and had once been the master of a gallant ship. In that important position he had been for many years a pleasant and popular officer; but at length, in an evil day, through some temporary weakness or neglect, he had lost his charge, and almost ruined his employers. The world—with what degree of truth cannot now be told—had charged the loss upon intoxication. A storm of obloquy and reproach arose. The man, bowed down with self-abasement and sensitiveness, had yielded to the blast, and attempted no defence; and, after awhile, obtaining, through some friendly influence, the custody of the Beacon Light, he had fled, with his child, to that obscurity, leaving no trace behind him, and caring only to pass the rest of his life in the quiet of the world's forgetfulness.

I was myself the occasional tenant of a lighthouse, for, during a few weeks of the summer, I had been visiting the Penguin Light, some four or five miles distant up the coast. It was a tall and far-reaching structure, standing upon a jutting point of rock— almost the duplicate of the Beacon Ledge; the two lights glimmering at each other across the little bay between, and only to be distinguished apart at night by the different periods of their revolutions. Penguin Light was in the keeping of old Barry Somers, a long-known and valued sailor-friend of mine, who, in past days, had taught me to swim, and sail a boat, and now seemed to regard his office more for the opportunity it gave of entertaining me than for its actual salaried value. Thither, therefore, I would often repair during the summer months, avoiding the usual crowded haunts, and giving preference to old Barry's pleasant talk and my solitary rambles along the shore; occasionally running out to sea, that I might speak friendly pilots cruising in the distance ; and now and then, by way of change and innocent attempt at usefulness, taking my turn at keeping up and watching over the safety of the lantern-lamps.

It was during one of my lonely wanderings along the beach, when, with gun in hand, I made feeble and unsuccessful attempts against the lives of the merry little sand-pipers, that I first saw Jessie. She sat upon a rock, and was gazing out at sea. In her hand was a book, which she was not reading —who, indeed, could read collectedly, with that fresh breeze lifting such a pleasant array of dancing white-caps, and rolling inward those strong bodies of surf, which broke upon the shore with the ring of sportive Titans? Her handkerchief had fallen off her head, and her curls were flying wantonly in the breeze. I did not, for the moment, dream that she had any connection with the lighthouse, but rather that she was a chance city visitor at some inland country-house; and so I passed on, not venturing to speak with her. So, also, the next day, and the next—finding her always there when I passed, as though that particular hollow in the rock was her own especial, allotted refuge-place. At last, gaining courage from those frequent meetings, and, perhaps, from the half smile with which she began to greet my coming, I addressed her ; and so the few words of salutation gradually lengthened into conversation, and, before we were well conscious of the fact, had ripened into terms of intimacy.

How swiftly such matters sometimes proceed, when removed from the stiffness and ceremony of city life ! A week only had passed, and I began to find that all my walks led in that one direction. Jessie was always at her place, with the uncompleted book in her hands ; and I, going no farther, would seat myself beside her, throw down my useless gun, let the poor sand-pipers go undismayed, and so prepare for the comfortable, pleasant conversation of the morning. It was no unattractive pastime, indeed, to dispose the dry sea-weed for her seat ; and then, placing my head upon another pile, remain half reclined at her feet, listening to her lively talk, and pretending to look out upon the blue waves, when, all the while, I was stealthily gazing into the deeper blue of her eyes. Nor, when I heard her story—or, so much of it as at first she deigned to tell me—did I hold her in less respect. The daughter of the lighthouse, indeed ! Why, truly, this should matter nothing at all to me. What interest could I have in her past or present associations, or how could they, in any way, detract from her own native grace and loveliness ? Were her eyes less bright, or was her conversation less

cheery, or were her attitudes less picturesque and
pleasing, because old Captain Barkstead, instead of
still sailing a fleet merchantman, now mopingly
cleaned his reflectors, and, when strangers came,
hid himself in the lantern? Moreover, had she
not brought with her from her former home, wherever that might be, a wit, and intellect, and intelligence which might adorn any position? What
more could be needful in promotion of a quiet sea-
side flirtation? In a week or ten days I should go
away, and no longer see her. I should carry off
with me the memories of a very pleasant face, that
had always brightened up whenever I came near;
and then, as, after awhile, new forms and scenes
came between, I would, of course, forget her. For
a time, she might possibly look out longingly after
my return, and, finding that I did not come back,
might—well, not exactly lose memory of me, I
hoped. It was to be desired, perhaps, that a few
thoughts of me would always tinge her future life,
I argued with something of man's selfishness. I
would not, indeed, that she should make herself
miserable about me ; but if, when her face had faded
from my thoughts, some little record of myself
should pleasantly remain with her, and now and
then bring a transitory pang of musing regret, who
should say nay?

Therefore, in time, I went away. I did not steal
off without farewell. That would have been
but sorry recompense for the many cheery hours
she had given me. But, taking her hand in mine,

I gave to her my heartfelt thanks for all the pleasant past, and my cordial wishes for the future. I
did not know that I should ever meet her again, I
said. I hoped, however, that she would not too
soon forget me. It was in my heart to utter more
tender and sentimental words than I had any right
to use, but I repressed the inclination. I cherished,
too a secret hope that she would show some sorrow
for my departure ; but, if she felt any at all, she did
not allow her expression, or her color, to betray
her. With quiet self-possession, yet with a certain
interest, too—as when one gives up a pleasant, valued friend—she bade me adieu ; and so, lifting
from her feet the ever-harmless gun, I passed away,
round the border of the little bay, and returned to
the city.

There, however, somewhat to my surprise, I
failed to forget her; and wherever I went, the
image of that light, graceful form, seated upon
the rock, began to obtrude itself upon my thoughts.
Of course, it was only a fleeting impression, I rea-
soned with myself, and would soon disappear again,
as newer scenes and faces forced themselves upon
me ; and I plunged rather more wildly than usual
into society. But the proposed remedy did not
have its due effect. In fact, it happened that the
routine of gayety and formality seemed, by contrast, to aid the former impressions, making them
seem more real and life-like than ever. It could
not be that I was falling in love! But yet I could
not fail to confess a strange interest ; and, while

knowing that I was in danger, was content to let myself drift whither the current might carry me.

"I will see her once more. There was something I forgot to tell her when we parted last," I said to myself, trying in vain to establish and believe in a transparent self-deceit. "It was about a book, or something. It weighs upon my mind that she should deem me neglectful of her wishes. Once more, therefore, and then—"

"Where away, so late in the autumn?" inquired a friend, who saw me starting out.

"Down the bay, blue-fishing!" I exclaimed. "Just the real time for it."

"Ah? Well, good-by, then! Rather too cold sport for me, though!"

Therefore, I saw Jessie again—and yet again after that. Why should I not confess it?—or, after what I have already told, what is there left for me to confess, at all? For now, at last, I began to acknowledge to myself that it was not mere friendship or esteem I felt, but, rather, the more overpowering passion of real love. Gone, like a thin veil of vapor, were all my sophistries about a limited Platonic interest; my dread of incongruous association; my resolves against possible rashnesses; my fear of the world or its senseless gossip; my prudence, or my self-restraint! These all seemed to vanish in a day; and, yielding myself, slavishly, a willing captive to bright eyes and silvery tones, upon one fine morning I passed the Rubicon of safety, and offered her my hand

and heart. But, to my sore dismay, she only softly shook her head.

"You do not love me, then?" I murmured. I spoke not merely with sorrow and disappointment, but with something of wounded pride — feeling mortified that she had not at once accepted my devotion. Certainly, it had seemed to me, all along, that I was not disagreeable to her ; and there was no doubt that in her manner, at least, she had always cordially welcomed my approach, and taken pleasure in my company.

"I do not know—I hardly yet can tell!" she faintly said, drawing her hand from mine. "To me, you are my best and dearest friend ; perhaps, the only one whom I can really call my friend. I know how glad I always feel when you come hither ; how lonely I am while you stay away. But this I do not think is love—the real, true love which I should wish to feel."

"But can it never be?" I pleaded.

"How can I tell? It might come to that, at last ; and yet—" She ceased, and there came over her face a strange, dead look at the sea before her —a straining gaze, as though she would fix her eyes far beyond, in another hemisphere, oblivious of the present.

"Yet tell me, Jessie, have I a rival? This, at least, you might let me know. I will not go further, nor will I ask his name."

For a moment she did not answer : still sitting, with that strange, rapt, straining gaze, and with an unconscious, mechanical motion, rolling the little sand pebbles down the side of the rock.

"There was one," she said, at length. "I hardly know how to tell you about it. I believe that I cared for him, and yet I never told him so; nor did he ever tell me that he loved or cared for me, and yet, at the time, I thought that he did. It was some time ago—a very long time, it often seems to me; nor do I suppose that he and I will ever meet again. And now you know almost as much about it as I do myself," she continued, turning more fully toward me. "Or what more can I say? There was no pledge given on either side—no uttered words—and, of course, it has all gone by. But now and then, when I think about it, I feel regret; and it seems to me as though it were a different and stronger feeling than that which I have for you. Whether I am mistaken in my feelings, or how or what I really think, perhaps I cannot well tell; I am only a simple girl, after all, and know so very little about love, or what love truly is."

"Yet, Jessie dear," I pleaded, "if you look upon that old matter as buried and gone—which, doubtless, it must be—why think longer about it, instead of turning to the new and truer affection which now I offer you? Believe me, you are letting your mind dwell merely upon a dream of the past—one of those vain fancies of girlhood, which, though for the time they may control the mind, have no real, vital activity or force."

"It may be so," she said, in a sort of saddened, half-regretful tone. "Indeed, it must be so ; and it might be that when the influence has passed away, I may find that I have cared for you better than I have imagined. I know that, even now, you seem dear to me as a friend, and that you are kind to me, making me always happy at your coming ; yet, at the same time, I think that there is something wanting in it all—something which is not love. You see that I am very plain with you. Better, then, to leave me ; is it not so ? For I cannot now give you my heart ; nor do I know whether, in the future, I can better do so ; and it is not right that I should keep you at my side, hoping or expecting what, after all, may never come."

"Nay, I will not leave you for all that, my Jessie," I said, impulsively. "I will still remain at your side, and trust even to the mere chance that, at some future period, you may relent."

Therefore, dropping the subject for that time, I remained, and sought, by new kindnesses and attentions, to win some final increase of her favor toward me, but feeling, at the same time, a little sore and angry with myself. For, how wretchedly was I now maintaining that proper independence of spirit, which I had always insisted even the most blinded and devoted of lovers should feel ! Had it not been my cherished theory that no man should surrender his freedom of heart without obtaining in return the utmost, unlimited, and unselfish devotion ? Yet, here I was giving up my whole soul to a blind passion, rendered more and more absorbing, doubtless, by the opposition I experienced, and for response I found myself willing to be content with even the cinders of a former and only half-dead affection ; trusting, as so many men have vainly trusted, that by earnest care and assiduity, I might, at last, re-illume the fading spark, and make its new brightness glow for me.

So passed the autumn, during which I made frequent journeys between coast and city ; striving, at times, with the cares of business to drive her image from my mind, and finding myself continually drawn back again to that quiet nook which, gifted with her presence, had become to me the brightest and only happy spot on earth. ·These frequent departures, so contrary to my usual habit, soon began to excite the inquiries and surmises of my friends. Fishing and shooting protracted into the season so far as almost to touch the edge of the winter, no longer served as satisfactory excuses for my absences ; and there were some among my friends, who, in their speculations, came very near the truth, and hinted suspicions of some rustic passion. But still, turning off their insinuations with a laugh, I kept my secret—holding it the more carefully and earnestly, as I now began to see hope dawning for me in the future.

For now, at last, it seemed as if I was about to prosper in my suit. Each time that I came, Jessie appeared yet more pleased to see me—more willing to give me that attractive confidence which can only exist in full perfection between acknowledged lovers ; less disposed to analyze her mind's emotion with any critical severity, or speculate whether this or that feeling had, or had not, passed the line between friendship and love; more ready, at times, to surrender the struggle and self-examination, confess herself vanquished, and yield up her whole heart to my keeping. But not quite yet.

" A little longer," she pleaded. " Let me feel somewhat more sure of myself before—"

" And how much longer, then, Jessie ?"

" Till Christmas, George. When Christmas comes, I will either be all your own, or will send you away forever. Will not that do ?"

" It must, perforce, if I cannot gain better terms," I answered ; and I returned once more to my city life. It was my fixed intention to remain there resolutely until the Christmas morning itself had come ; but at last, unable to maintain the suspense, I stole back to the beach once more. It was now only two days from the time. The air was colder, of course, so that Jessie no longer took her place outside upon the rock ; but we could sit and talk in the shelter of the lighthouse door, undisturbed by old Barkstead, who usually fretted and moped out of sight, about half way up the shaft.

" Only two days more, dear Jessie," I said, " and then— Will it be well with me, do you think ?"

"I think—I begin to think it will be well," she said, looking away.

"Then, if so you think, why should you longer delay your choice?" I pleaded.

"Nay, George, it is only two days more. Let it, then, remain as first we said, and we shall be the better satisfied at having held out to the proper end."

Gaining nothing more from her, but feeling, in my own mind, well assured of ultimate success, I prepared to depart. Not to return to the city, indeed, for that would scarcely be worth while for such a little interval—but to the Penguin Light, where Barry Somers, as usual, had a place ready for me. But, as I was leaving, a sudden idea struck me—a wild, foolish fancy, it might be—yet, coming, as it did, with a certain investiture of originality, it fastened itself firmly and tenaciously upon me, and with animation I returned upon my steps.

"Listen, dear Jessie!" I said. "Until Christmas morning, therefore, I will not see you again, for I do not wish thus vainly to renew my pleadings, and it will be pleasanter to know that when I meet you once more, it will be with sweet confession on your lips, and the permission to look upon you thenceforward as my own. But still, while we are thus separated, can we not commune together?"

"How, George?"

"With the lights, dear Jessie. See here, now!

Mark how easily we can arrange our signalling, so that, across the intervening miles, we can flash our secret intelligence, and no one but ourselves be the wiser ! Look !—I will now write you out some signs, and with them, at night, we will hold our intercourse. This very evening I will control the lamps at Penguin Light, and you shall read what I will therewith tell you. To-morrow you will answer me from here ; and I, in turn, will decipher your sweet words. Will not that be a rare, as well as pleasant correspondence ?''

At the suggestion, her eyes brightened up with animated excitement, and at once she prepared to second my plan. How, indeed, could a young girl help approving of such a novel conception ? To talk with beacon-lights across five miles of foaming, heaving waters, when all around was dark and dreary !—to flash from one sympathetic heart to another the glowing signals of intelligence comprehended by no other persons ! — would not that be an achiévement which would not only give pleasure in the actual present performance of it, but also in the recollection of it throughout future years ? So, sitting down again, she eagerly listened to me, while I, drawing a paper from my pocket, noted down the requisite tokens, something after the usual signs employed in ordinary telegraphy— short and simple—and left them in her possession. I saw at once that she comprehended the principle ; so, feeling no doubt that she would well perform

her part, I departed, reading, in her pleased consciousness of sharing that novel secret with me,
such probable indications of affection, that, for the
moment, I could scarcely resist once more throw-
ing myself upon her pity, and asking instant assur-
ance of my happiness.

But I forbore. Were I now to win her, in anticipation of that predetermined Christmas-day,
might it not take something from the zest of the
coming midnight correspondence?

So, controlling myself, I returned to Penguin
Light. I had been a little troubled with the idea
that, perhaps, I might not be able to manage the
matter, after all; but, almost to my joy, I found
old Barry complaining of his rheumatism, hobbling
about, and looking wrathfully up the winding
stairs, in surly deprecation of his approaching
ascent. Upon which I seized the favorable opportunity, and, while relieving him, forwarded my
own views.

"Let it alone for this night, Barry. Do you
stay down here and make yourself comfortable,
and I will keep watch in the lantern, and tend the
lights."

"And can you keep awake, Georgy, my boy, do
you think?"

"Of course I can, Barry."

Whereupon, for sole answer, Barry stumped
away into the closet below—which he called his
room—laid himself carefully away upon his old
blankets, and I mounted to the lantern. There—

the hour of sundown having come—I lighted the lamps, and awaited my time. That was still some hours off ; I was to do nothing until midnight. Meanwhile, I laid myself down to take a nap. I had promised watchfulness, but it was hardly necessary in the beginning of the night. The wicks were then fresh, and it was not likely that any accident could happen. It was only toward the end of the night, when the wicks might become incrusted or the reflectors dimmed, that especial care was needed.

I awoke again about midnight, the hour ap-_ pointed for the commencement of my feat. The sky had clouded over, and not a star was to be seen. All the better, indeed, for the experiment ; for now there was no light to be seen in any direction, except where down the coast glimmered the Beacon Ledge Beacon—now faintly coming around the side, then glowing for a second like the mouth of a distant furnace, as its full focus of reflectors was pointed directly at me, then fading away, and so, for an instant, entirely disappearing, as it turned slowly toward the south. With the thick bank of clouds had come a cold wind from the north, premonitory of an approaching storm, though it might be days before it reached us—the only change to be now noted being the somewhat heavier swell of the surf, rolling up with a dull, sullen roar along the curve of the rock-bound shore.

I prepared for action. As I sat in the lantern,

the great brazen frame of polished reflectors swung around, once in each minute, within a few inches of the side. Beneath was the projecting handle of a crank, or lever, by pressing upon which the revolution could be instantly arrested. Stooping down, I could sit at ease, with my head clear from any contact with the lamps, and in that position could have the lever-handle within easy reach.

Waiting for a moment until the reflectors pointed directly toward Beacon Ledge, I pressed upon the crank, and thereby suspended the revolution. Thus inert and motionless I held the machinery for a full minute, and then, lifting the rod, allowed the circuit to recommence, and gazed anxiously toward the other lighthouse. For a moment, no response; but then, as its reflectors came slowly around and pointed toward me, they, too, ceased in their motion for a full minute. With that my heart exulted. . My signal for conversation had been seen and answered. So far, all went satisfactorily, and there was nothing left but to commence the main business of the night.

What should I talk to Jessie about? I could not frame any lengthy sentences, indeed—for that, time and patience would not suffice. Nor could I tell her any especial piece of news : all such matters had already been discussed between us. Nor did it seem any thing but ridiculous to repeat, in such a labored manner, any of the ordinary commonplaces about health, or the time, or weather. The most I could do, in fact, would be to telegraph some short and simple idea, expressive of my affection for her, and of my ardent faith in its coming realization. This she would comprehend, and, like a proverb, it would tell, in brief, a whole long story.

Watching until the reflectors again came round, I seized the lever, held the machinery in suspense for a whole minute, and then set it free again. Another circuit, and this time I arrested the motion for only fifteen seconds. A third, and here again a suspension of a whole minute. In this way, by putting the three circuits together, I had contrived to spell out the letter C—as in a telegraph office the operator would write a letter, though probably not the same one, with a long, a short, and a long scratch upon the paper slip.

Again : and now I let the reflectors remain stationary, first, for a minute, then twice for fifteen seconds each. This—a long, and two short arrestations—spelled the letter H. So, little by little, I wrote out with the lighthouse flash against the dark sky the simple sentence,

" Christmas is coming."

It was plain and expressive. It spoke to Jessie of the approaching day, when she should make her long-deferred decision, and when I so ardently anticipated that she would be mine. It reminded her that the time was now only a few hours distant. It told her that even those few hours were almost too long for me to wait. It was a short message, indeed, but the difficulty of thus spelling it out, letter by letter, made it long enough. Already, ere I had finished, my arm, as well as my attention, was fatigued ; and when, at last, I made the long signal of conclusion, and gained, in reply, the token that I had been comprehended, I felt that I had done enough for one night, at least.

Then, remaining awake, with some difficulty, until morning came, I put out the lights, and went down to see after old Barry. He was better ; his rheumatism had not troubled him as much as he had feared ; he would get up, and himself trim the lights for the coming night, and I had better lie down and rest. Which I gladly did, for I was tired, indeed, and began to have a suspicion that, though lighthouse telegraphy might be a pleasant excitement for once, it was inferior, as a steady means of communication, to the regularly established mails. So, I slept the sleep of the weary, if not of the just ; and the morning was far advanced when I awoke.

The new day was not stormy, as I had partly anticipated it would be, nor yet was it clear and beautiful. The gale seemed slowly coming on, but had not quite reached us. The sky was thick with scudding clouds, racing wildly from north to south ; the air was cold and cheerless ; the sea rolled in with a more powerful swell than usual, breaking along the shore with a boom like that of heavy artillery. The gulls flew to and fro, screaming and unsettled ; a few coasting schooners, apprehensive of mischief, had put into the land-locked bay and there lay at anchor, awaiting better weather ; and in one place, the fishermen were dragging their boats away back to the foot of the bluff, so as to avoid the still heavier swell which must erelong come. Yet, for all that, the storm had not commenced, and I could easily have walked over to Beacon Ledge and made my daily visit.

But still I forbore. I had already told Jessie that I should not see her again until I came to hear the decision of my fate, and I resolved that I would be firm. Would it not, beside, spoil the whole romance of our midnight correspondence were I to visit her again so soon ? I had signalled a greeting to her. What a lowering of sentiment it would be if now I were to obtain her response in commonplace manner, by mere word of mouth, instead of by the bright sheen of the lighthouse itself ! Nay, that would never do. So, killing the heavy hours as best I could, I loitered up and down the beach, shooting at the gulls as ineffec-tually as I had before shot at the sand-pipers ; watching the course of a few frightened vessels, which still continued to make for that little harbor of refuge ; and, like a child, making sand-forts on the beach, for the pleasure of seeing them washed away again by the next heavy swell.

Night came at last ; and, as before, I volunteered to relieve Barry of the care of the lamps, and

allow him additional opportunity to nurse his
rheumatism.   As before, he made some feeble show
of hesitation, by way of reconciling his mind to
the proffered rest, and then readily succumbed.

"Be it so, Georgy, my boy," he said.   "That
is, if you are not already too tired.   But I don't
feel as bad now as last night, and may yet crawl
up and relieve you."

"Take it easy, Barry," I said.   "It is not much
trouble for me.   I could stand it this fashion for a
week."

With that I left him alone in his snuggery, and
climbed the stairs to the top.   As upon the previous
evening, I lighted the lamps, set the machine in motion, and then curled myself down in a corner of the
floor to rest till midnight.   I did not at once fall
asleep, however.   The gale, which had been pre-
paring for the last thirty hours, now began to come
in force, disturbing me with the sound of the wind
—whistling shrilly through every crack and crevice
—while the lighthouse itself constantly trembled
with the blast.   Even at that height, I could hear
the sullen dash of the breakers against the shore ;
and once I could see, by the tremulous movement
of lights far out to the eastward, that a large
steamer was passing, and was laboring toilsomely
with a more than usually heavy sea.   She was in
no danger, however, and gradually passed away
from my line of vision.   Then, at last, I fell
asleep, though not into the soft, quiet slumber
which I usually enjoyed.   Even in my dreams the

tempest followed me, filling my mind with distorted imaginings. The old stories, which I had so often heard and of late had forgotten, about pirates, and wrecks, and wreckers, and cruelties perpetrated upon the beach, now seemed to take actual life and reality. I could see the dismasted vessels struggling among the breakers, and the rows of hard, fierce, expectant faces lining the shore, and awaiting the turning up of the dead bodies. I was a dead body myself, even, and was being washed up on the beach, already drowned beyond hope of resuscitation, and yet strangely conscious of all that went on around me. A hand was placed roughly upon me, as I lay motionless upon the sand. Then, gaining new life, I cried aloud, and, waking, found old Barry leaning over me, and shaking me into consciousness.

"Look over yonder, Georgy, my boy, at the Beacon Point," he said. "See how strangely the lights are acting. What do you make of it all?"

I looked, and saw that the reflectors were pointing, motionless, toward me—resting there for a full minute; then they swept around slowly in their accustomed course, and again paused for a minute. Thereby I deciphered the letter M, and started into full and instant animation. I had, of course, overslept myself, and thereby, probably, lost a portion of Jessie's dear message. How much of it, indeed?

"What is the hour, Barry?"

"Half-past twelve," he said. "But what do

you make of yonder business ?   Is it some accident
to the works, do you think ?—or has old Barkstead gone on a spree again, as they say he once
did, and is now playing fast and loose with the
lights ?''

While he had been speaking, new revolutions,
broken, ·by longer or shorter pauses, had succeeded ; and I deciphered the additional letters
A and S.

"Whatever it may be, Barry," I then answered
—forcing myself to attend to him, and feeling a
little guilty for being obliged to keep the mysterious secret from him—" don't you see that nothing can be done about it, now ?   Go, therefore, to
bed again.   This cold lantern is no place for you
to remain in.   And to-morrow, bright and early,
I will go out myself, and ascertain what may be
the matter."

With that, I gently pushed Barry down the first
two or three steps, and heard him go grumbling
and puffing the rest of the way to his own nook.
Meanwhile, the bright signalling from Beacon Point
went on—letter after letter—until, at last, I read
out the whole sentence :

"——*mas has come.*"

"Christmas has come !"   This, of course, was
the completion of the message ; for it was not now
difficult to supply those letters which, through my
tardy   awakening,   I   had   missed.   My   heart

bounded high with joy and exultation. Sanguinely as I had anticipated a favorable verdict at Jessie's hands, my utmost hopes had never asked for such a frank and instant admission of her preference as this. To be reminded, at the very first stroke of the midnight hour, that the important day for decision had arrived : what was this but being told that the day should bring its blessing with it?—that Jessie herself had awaited its approach as eagerly as I had, feeling as acutely the delay ?—that now there should be no more disguise or misconstruction between us ? Christmas had come ! It was, indeed, a frank and noble response to my message of the night before, telling me that now, at last, she had surrendered her heart to my safe-keeping. Had it been possible, I would have run over at once to' Beacon Ledge, and pressed her to my heart. But, of course, not the tempest merely forbade. I must wait until the more suitable time of morning, still many hours off. Therefore, composing myself as well as possible for quiet waiting, I sat, during the remainder of the night, musing over my pleasant prospects, and watching anxiously for the first ray of morning.

It came at last—later than usual, for the tempest had not yet abated, and the approach of day was to be noted rather by the gradual lightening of the atmosphere, than by any gleam of eastern dawn. Then I extinguished the lights, stopped the machinery, and descended to old Barry.

"I will now cross over to the Beacon Ledge," I
said, "and find out what was the matter last
night."

"Without your breakfast, boy?" growled the
old man.

But what did I care for breakfast! My heart
was too full of joy to care for any carnal needs;
and, therefore, with some lame excuse for my
hurry, and a guilty sense of continued deception
weighing upon my mind, I set off, promising a
speedy return. The task that I had set myself was
no trifle, and I could not wonder at the solemn
shake of the head with which Barry watched my
departure. The tempest was at its height, and a
blinding sheet of rain and ocean-spray drove wildly
into my face at each step. The breakers dashed
furiously upon the beach—so furiously, indeed,
that the usual route along the hard-pressed sand
had become impassable, and I was obliged to take
a higher path through the loose, yielding pebbles.
But I persevered bravely and determinedly, though
so sorely fettered in my steps, and buffeted in my
face, and, after nearly two hours, reached the other
lighthouse.

I entered without ceremony, and, in the angle of
the first flight of stairs—our usual trysting-place
ever since the lateness of the season had denied us
the rock by the sea-side—I found dear Jessie. But
she was not alone. Beside her, and too near, I
thought, sat a pleasant-faced young man, who, at
my approach, arose, and with a miserably counter-

feited affectation of indifference, sauntered away.
Jessie also arose, and with whitened face, came forward.

" Why are you here ?" she murmured. " Did I
not signal it all to you, so that you might know
the truth, and spare both yourself and me this
meeting ?"

" What do you mean ?" I gasped.

" Did you not understand me, after all, kind
friend ? You know, indeed, that I once told you
how I had loved another. I had no expectation of
seeing him again, it is true. He was far away
with his vessel when we departed from our little
village, leaving, as you know, not a trace behind
us ; and, therefore, there was no way in which the
secret of our present retreat could be learned by
any one. Nor could I write to him and tell him,
for he had not yet spoken to me of love, and I did
not know but what he would choose, in the end,
to forget me. But Fate, after all, is sometimes
kind. Searching for me, without any trace to guide
him, he had almost despaired, when, the night
before this last, coming in from sea, he saw the
Penguin Light ; and noticing how, while you were
signalling to me, at times it stopped for a moment,
he thought it was the Upper Roadstead Light, and
so ran in and made this little harbor by mistake.
Thereby it was that we have chanced to meet
again."

" But, Jessie, you signalled to me that—"

" I signalled that Thomas had come. Did you

not comprehend ? Or can it be that I had never happened to mention his name to you ?"

"Ah !" I feebly exclaimed, the light breaking in upon me ; " Thomas was the word, then, was it ? I thought—but no matter now for my thoughts. Well, farewell, Jessie. There can be no good word or wish that any one may give you that will not always be uttered twofold from my heart. You know it, kind friend, do you not ?"

" I know it, George, indeed," she said.

And, tearing myself from her, I returned to city life. There I gave myself once more up to business and its cares, in hopes of drowning my disappointment ; and now, after long months of sad regret, I have nearly succeeded, and have become myself again. But, at times, I lie awake in the middle of the night and listen to the city's roar, and in the sound I seem to hear once more the play of breakers on the shore at Beacon Ledge ; and then I think, with sadness, how different might have been my lot, had I not so foolishly determined to utter, with the lighthouse lamps, and so many miles across, those words of greeting which should have been softly whispered instead, by lowly pleading lips, into closely attentive, willing ears.